Cupid Files:
Elves Gone Wild

T. Lynne Tolles

Cupid Files – Elves Gone Wild
Troll Publishing

Prologue

The silvery moon glowed brightly between the dense clouds of a chilly night, encouraging those who longed for a white Christmas. Two excited children were being tucked into their warm beds by a white-haired, loving matriarch. Once she had them snug as two bugs in a rug, she asked them, "Have I ever told you the story about the year there was almost no Christmas?"

"Oh, Grandma...Santa would never let anything like that happen," the older girl stated.

"Sometimes things happen that are quite out of our control. Even Santa has day-to-day problems like the rest of us."

"Isn't Santa coming tonight, Grandma?" the youngest asked in distress.

"As far as I know, he's coming, but there was one year he wasn't so sure if the children of the world be so lucky."

"What happened?" the youngest replied.

"Well, let me tell you. It was a long time ago..."

Chapter One

He peeked from behind the thin sheets of newspaper he held up between them in a guise of reading, but mostly in an attempt to hide, much like an ostrich, knowing that he was fully visible.

His wife, the one he was hiding from, hit, smashed and beat the gingerbread dough onto the board, which he knew was her way of working off pent-up frustrations. With every punch, he winced. It was just a matter of time before she brought up the subject he hoped to avert for as long as possible, for in him beat the heart of a procrastinator, especially when it meant confrontation.

"You know, dear..." she started.

Oh no. The time had come. He tried to play it casual, still obscured by the newspaper he used as a shield. He mumbled some kind of grunt that was meant to be an acknowledgment of her statement.

"You really need to do something about those elves."

There it was—the subject he'd hoped not to deal with had landed at his feet. He hated reprimanding the elves. Their selfless servitude made it hard to scold them even if necessary. His mind whirred with the image of hundreds of their little faces staring up at him and jumping to any task he put before them. He sat frozen in apprehension. Then she continued, which made it worse.

"It's just not right what they've done to those polar bears."

His mind flooded with pictures of the colorful assortment of mohawks, a good ten inches wide, running from tail to eyebrows, leaving the rest of the bear a grayish black of hairless goose flesh. A very strange sight indeed, especially if one didn't know polar bears had black skin under all that white fur.

A quick journey to the south, Clara brought back the largest parkas made in the human world for the half-frozen bears. The store didn't have enough, so she instructed the elves to make the rest in their spare time.

"What in the world has gotten into them?" she said, pulling out cookies that smelled like heaven from the oven.

He didn't know how to answer the question, so he remained silent, but she was right. They had been very odd of late. One things elves were not was mischievous and that trait made them loyal and dutiful in their work. But lately, they'd been a little—as his wife had put it—cuckoo.

"It's one thing to play a prank, but, well, look at you..." she said.

He wished he didn't, but he knew what she was referring to. Just a week ago, unidentified elves came into their living quarters and sliced up all his winter apparel. He'd been forced to wear his red thermal underwear underneath his Bermuda shorts and an authentic Hawaiian shirt from a vacation some fifteen years before. How did they know it was an elf?

The surveillance outside their door showed two elves armed with large silver scissors, hiding their faces from the camera, entered, and an hour later, left with trailing red velvet shreds, some adorned with white fur.

He'd written off the incident as a practical joke, a hazing, or some dare forced upon the two by their peers. His wife had been diligently trying to repair the heirloom red suit, but it was useless, and more fabric had to be ordered and flown north to them. He'd have to make do with his present attire.

The worst part of the entire fiasco was that the only shoes he had were thongs. When worn with socks, they gave him a horrible blister where the socks bunched up between his toes.

He heard her make her way to him and he knew what awaited. He finally dropped the paper to accept the warm gingerbread man cookie that sat patiently for him on a plate. He tried to avoid her gaze, but when he took a bite of the sweet morsel of goodness she'd baked, he couldn't help but smile with thankful gratitude.

She smiled back and pulled a business card from her apron pocket, handing it to him. He asked, "What's this?" before quickly depositing more of the scrumptious confection in his mouth.

"I think you should call him."

He looked from her concerned face to the card and noted the name. "Oh no. What is this?" he said, not believing his eyes.

"Now, don't make judgments," she rebutted.

"But, Clara, he's, he's...he's already got a job."

"I know, but he so wants to try his hand at this and I think, as his friend and colleague, you should give him the benefit of the doubt."

"He's Cupid, for god's sake. As it is, he prances around in, well, in his underwear."

"He doesn't prance, dear, and at least he's taken to 'underwear.' It was much worse when he wore only the diaper."

He shook his head, thinking back to those days. "How could I forget," he said.

"Well. Are you going to call him? Or shall I?" she said sternly, handing him another cookie to butter him up.

She knew him too well. He was so easily manipulated by the sweets she concocted. He quickly shoved the doughy goodness into his mouth and mumbled something that sounded like a defeated acceptance. *God, she's good.* She headed to the beeping alarm on the stove. *Definitely knows me too well*, he thought, leaving the room and reviewing the business card once again. "Pink, figures..." he said, noting the color.

He didn't look forward to calling Cupid, but at least by engaging Cupid to the task, he wouldn't have to confront the elves himself, so not all was lost. *Maybe this had its benefits*, though he couldn't think of a one.

He slipped galoshes over his flip-flop clad feet, making the bunched-up sock between his toes smart a bit. He pulled out his cell phone and referred to the pastel-colored card for Cupid's number as he made his way to the stables. His overshoes made the snow crunch under his feet as he walked past the statuesque-looking garden gnome.

He greeted it with, "How's it going, Norman?"

The gnome's head rose in a nod of acknowledgment, but no words came from the smirking lips of the little man with snow almost to his neck. They were a quiet sort, gnomes—always watching but seldom a word. But Norman, well, he made him feel uneasy—something about his frozen expression didn't sit right with him. Trying to put the thought out of his mind, he lifted the phone to his ear. He could hear ringing on the other end while he continued past the speechless, bearded humanoid.

"Cupid Investigations," a voice said on the other end.

"Cupid? It's Chris Kringle."

"Santa, what can I do you for?"

"Clara asked me to call you," he said as he stood by the large barn doors watching the snow gently fall from the dark gray sky. "We've been having some trouble with the," he cupped his hand over his mouth and the speaker and quietly said, "elves."

"Oh? What kind of trouble?"

He ducked inside, looking around to make sure he was alone before continuing. "Well, for lack of a better word, they've been rather impish."

"Now, that is strange elven behavior. Can you give me an instance?"

"Sure. There's the polar bears."

"Yes? What's wrong with the polar bears?"

"They've been shaved."

"Naked?"

"No. Maybe it would be better if you came and saw for yourself."

"Of course."

"But can you be discreet about why you're here?"

"I can. How about I come out tomorrow morning."

"That would be fine. And thank you."

"Thank you, Santa. You're my first paying customer."

"Let's not get ahead of ourselves here. We're not sure if we have a problem or not."

"Fine. We'll discuss things tomorrow, including my fee and my retainer."

"Whatever," he said, realizing he might have made a very, very large mistake.

The following morning, there was a knock at the door just as he sat to take a bite of the stack of fluffy pancakes slathered in butter and maple syrup. He knew who it was and shook his head as Clara answered the door.

"Cupid," he heard her greet him.

"Mrs. Kringle, a delight to see you as always, and that smell, what is that amazing smell?" Cupid said, entering.

"Oh, it's just a batch of monkey bread I made for Chris. Would you like some?"

He grumbled as he saw the eager nod of Cupid's head. He eyed Cupid as he deposited his fedora on the hat hook, revealing a shiny bald head trimmed from ear-to-ear with silver white fur that looked like earmuffs about to fall off the back of his head.

Next, he shed a camel-colored trench coat that served no source of warmth in the arctic and was decidedly only to reinforce his look of a private investigator. To Chris, he looked more like an unprepared streaker donning a pink union suit accessorized with a buttoned flap hiding his derriere. His quiver and bow he had with him and draped them over the finial on the back of the dining chair.

While Clara served him an overly large portion of monkey bread, Cupid said, "Santa, good morning."

Chris nodded and took another bite of his breakfast.

"Enjoy," Clara said, setting down the plate in front of Cupid.

"Looks wonderful, Mrs. Kringle," he said, rubbing his hands together in an attempt to get warm. "Cold up here."

"It gets that way in the arctic, Cupid. You might want to try wearing pants, might keep you warmer," Chris said a little too flippantly for Clara's liking as she gave him a scolding glare when she set down coffee for Cupid.

"You're a hoot, Santa. I love your sense of humor. I've missed it. Especially this wild ensemble you're donning. Is it Hawaiian Day here in the north?"

"No," Chris said, annoyed. "My closet was the scene of another incident where everything I own, but what you see me wearing, was sliced to shreds."

"Hmm. I see," Cupid said, licking his fingers and pulling a notebook from his quiver then jotting down notes.

"It is very festive looking," Cupid added to Chris's dismay. "Haven't seen you in quite a while," he pressed on. "Was it April?"

"Yes. The emergency meeting with the rest of the holiday crew regarding the Easter bunny's claim that the tooth fairy sneaked chocolate teeth into the baskets for the children in Timbuktu."

"Right. That tooth fairy...he's always trying to get noticed." Chris nodded and continued devouring his food.

"So, shall we talk numbers?"

"You having some financial difficulties, Cupid?" Chris asked.

"No. Why do you ask?"

"Just that you've mentioned money several times now, and we haven't even agreed there's a problem or that I want you to work for me."

"Chris," Clara reprimanded.

"Well," Chris retorted.

"No, Mrs. Kringle, Santa's right. We can crunch numbers later." Chris raised his brow and eyed Clara as if to say, "See?" but she was having none of it.

Cupid prattled on about nothing in particular until they both finished eating.

Backing away from the table, Chris said, "Maybe we should go see what it is that's got Clara in such a state that she felt we needed to call in a private investigator." Clara frowned at him, but Cupid seemed so delighted by the employment reference that he ignored any resonating tension between the couple.

"Yes. We should."

Chapter Two

Cupid spoke nonstop as the two men made their way across a knee-high blanket of snow that seemed to stretch on forever. No critters had ventured across it since last night's snow, keeping it pristine and perfect before they plowed through.

They headed for a giant red building not far off that looked to be a stable. They opened a gate and next to the post in the snow, a purple conical form protruded from the white. As Chris passed, he muttered something under his breath that sounded to Cupid to be a greeting to someone named Hermon.

The snow around the cone moved slightly, catching Cupid's attention for a second before Chris urged him on. At the door of the barn sat a sleigh hooked up to reindeer.

"Are we flying?" Cupid asked with excitement.

"No. Flying is only for Christmas Eve and emergencies," he said with a bite to his voice.

They climbed in, settled themselves, and Chris took the reins and made a clicking noise with his tongue indicating to the reindeer to engage. As they slid along the snow, the bells on the harnesses of the reindeer jingled in rhythm to their canter.

Cupid shivered next to him and had most of the lap blanket wrapped around himself. Chris, who was used to the coldness of the terrain, made do, though in Bermuda shorts and red long johns, he wasn't exactly without goose bumps.

"Where exactly are we going?" Cupid asked after about fifteen minutes.

"We're heading to the Lagoon of Ice."

"Sounds cold," Cupid said and Chris eyed him in annoyance, but decided not to mention his lack of preparedness for his investigation.

"Why there?" Cupid asked.

"That's where the bulk of our polar bears live. Thought it would be easier to show what has been done than to explain."

"Okay," Cupid said with hesitance.

It wasn't long before all uncertainty had been removed, for the sight before them was one a person could never forget. Fifteen or more parka-clad polar bears huddled together. What fur that was not shaved off in some kind of pattern was dyed fluorescent colors. Most had a mohawk, but others had patches of hair shaved into swirls, stars, polka dots and even words.

"Oh my God. What happened to them? They look like they were attacked by a crazy barber," Cupid said, gawking at the sight before him.

"We have it on good word that this is the work of rogue elves."

"But how? Polar bears are deadly and huge."

"They were drugged with sleeping pills in a meal of a washed-up whale."

"And the parkas?"

"That was Clara's doing."

"Good thinking."

"She's a kind soul."

"Indeed."

"Despite the drugs, there are a lot of bare bears. There had to be more than just the two elves who shredded your clothes that did this job."

"That's my thought, too."

"It's so unlike elves to be malicious."

"And that is why you're here. The workshop is nearly at a standstill. This is NOT just a few rogue elves. This seems to be affecting most if not all of them. With fall upon us, the shop needs be ramping up to full capacity by Halloween and that's next week. Clearly, we're not at that point, and there is no hint that whatever is happening is on the decline."

"I'd say not," Cupid said, re-examining the color mob of bare-bottomed bears.

"I would like you to find out what is going on here as quickly as you can so we can rectify it. Whether it's disgruntlement or an epidemic, we need to stop it and get on with business as usual or there won't be a Christmas this year."

"Right. We can't have that. I'll get on it right away."

"Good. And as for money...there is none. We're nonprofit, just like all the other holiday folks. You know that, but the elves can make you whatever you want when this is solved."

"Sounds like a deal."

"Great. Time's a-wastin'. Let's get back and let you start...whatever it is you do."

"Right you are, Santa. Don't you worry. Cupid P.I. is at your service."

Santa rolled his eyes but was thankful and patted Cupid on the back as they got into the sleigh.

Back at the village, Cupid and Chris found themselves watching an oncoming sight that seemed to have everyone in a panic. It looked to be a person upon the smallest looking snowmobile ever built, but in actuality, it was the person's massiveness that dwarfed the vehicle.

As it grew closer, the whine of the engine became deafening. It was Hilda from the ATP—Arctic Troll Patrol, the law around these parts. She stopped just short of them and a wave of snow projected forward, almost completely covering Cupid in a mound of the icy powder. She deftly hopped off the contraption and spoke with Chris, not batting an eye to the mess she'd made of Cupid.

"Santa, sir."

"Hilda. What brings you here?"

"Trouble, sir."

"Oh?"

"Yes. Someone keeps moving the North Pole."

"I'm sorry, what?" Cupid said, brushing white flakes from himself. "You can't move the pole. It's impossible."

"Not the actual pole, obviously, but the man-made reproduction that signifies where the pole resides unseen. The one everyone comes here to see and take a picture next to," she explained in a squeaky, high-pitched voice Cupid never imagined a woman of such ruggedness and size could ever possess.

"Oh, I see," he said, back-pedaling a bit.

"Why would anyone do such a thing?" Chris asked.

"I'd say a prank, but this is a bit more than that," she said, eyeing Cupid with her cool, shocking-blue eyes before showing a picture on her phone to Chris.

His response was, "Oh my. That is a problem. Show him," Chris directed. She looked puzzled by his instructions, but Chris continued. "Cupid, here, is helping with 'our' problem."

She handed the phone to Cupid, sizing him up as she did. Cupid was astonished by what he saw on the phone. *I definitely have to check this out in person later,* he thought to himself.

"Help? What kind of help?" she inquired.

"Cupid, this is Hilda, our local law enforcer."

"That's right. And that's Ms. Rocke to you, Mr. Cupid," she said. "What makes you think I need help, Santa, sir?"

"I don't. I just need this problem with the elves, whatever it is, to stop—yesterday. An extra set of eyes and ears couldn't hurt, could it?" Chris said.

She didn't look convinced. "So what is he?" she asked.

"I," Cupid said, "am a private investigator," and offered his hand in greeting. She didn't accept it and he was left with his hand between them feeling awkward.

"Isn't Cupid a matchmaker fairy or something?" she said to Chris while pointing to Cupid's wings and bow.

"I am not a fairy. I'm a cherub, which, I might add, is nothing like a fairy. They can be such mean little creatures," he said, trailing off on that thought.

"Sorry," she chuckled. "He's kind of sensitive," she pretended to whisper to Chris, elbowing him in the ribs. "I don't need any sissy-fied, bald cherub in pink underwear getting in the way of my investigation," she claimed.

"He won't be in the way. He'll just, you know, investigate. Quietly. And quickly," Chris reiterated.

"No. I don't do well with partners. Besides, look at him, he'll never survive the night in that get up."

"I will, too," Cupid said, insulted by her comments.

"Fine. He will investigate, and you will investigate. Neither of you will get in each other's way."

"He better not. But if by chance he does find something pertinent, I expect full disclosure. I'm the law, after all."

Cupid interrupted and voiced his misgivings, but it fell on deaf ears. Before he got another word in, the conversation was over and the mammoth of a woman was back upon her horrendously loud snowmobile and gone.

"So we're good?" Chris asked.

Cupid only smirked at him and headed off to find lodging and a warmer coat.

A couple online searches, and Cupid was able to find bibbed snow pants in a dashing red and a hot pink parka rated for extreme cold weather, and surprisingly marked quite reasonably. He had them shipped overnight to the Candy Lane Lodge where he was staying.

It was a nice place, though most of its clientele was under four foot in height, making for a few minor problems for a man five foot ten, but the employees were very accommodating and quickly pushed two elfin-king beds together and supplied him with as many helpings as he wanted when it came to food.

His biggest problem was the door height. He'd hit his forehead on the header of the door casing every time he went through a door, and his noggin was littered with different-sized Band-Aids.

The good thing was that the restaurant within seemed to be a meeting hub for the elves, giving him access to eavesdropping on their conversations, though he was anything but inconspicuous. It was hard to blend in amongst a crowd of people a good foot or two shorter. Cupid was up to the challenge and spent a great deal of time behind a copy of the *North Pole Times*, checking notes in his memo pad, eating cookies, and reading his go-to guide for sleuthing, *So You Want to Be a Detective*.

Despite his efforts, there was nothing really to report. There was plenty of talking about toy making, but none of the height-challenged people seemed to be unhappy with their working conditions. It was mostly discussions on better ways to engineer things or speed up the process. When they weren't talking, they were nodding off, face-planted on the table or sitting up, head wobbling to and fro, snoring up a storm.

Cupid turned to a clean page in his journal of notes and crossed off the word "Disgruntled?" on his list headlined "Motives" and scribbled a note "very tired, why?" in the margin.

They seemed a happy folk for the most part—enjoying life as it was. He looked at his list again and none of the motives he had written down deemed plausible—Jealousy, Revenge, Financial gain. This wasn't going to be your run-of-the-mill case. And as he contemplated that and looked at the other columns, "Suspects" and "Incidents," in walked Ms. Rocke of the Arctic Troll Patrol. *Swell*, he thought.

"Kewpie," she addressed the waitress, "I have an order to go."

"Yes. One minute, Hilda," she answered and headed back to the kitchen.

"If it isn't the Mr. Fancy pants detective. How's your investigation going? Working hard, are you?" she greeted him loudly, noting his plate of cookies and his How-To book. Every elf that wasn't sawing logs turned to look at Cupid with a scowl.

Realizing the elves would now have their guards up whenever he was around, he stammered, "Well, it was fine until just a moment ago."

"Oh, you mean I blew your cover?" she pretended to whisper.

"Very droll, Ms. Rocke. I thought we weren't going to get in one another's way."

"I'm just here to pick up some dinner. No toes under these feet," she said, looking at her ice-covered boots.

"Yes. You're very clever. I think I'll take my leave now," he said, gathering up his items, and with a moment's hesitation, he grabbed the recently replenished plate of cookies and stomped past her toward the stairs.

"Don't leave on my account," she teased.

He turned to give her one more unappreciative glare when he ran his head into the header of the doorway, making most of the room laugh and Cupid feel even more humiliated.

"You ought to duck at the doorways, there, or there's not going to be a patch on your head that doesn't have a bandage on it!" she yelled, laughing after him. He grumbled and went upstairs.

Chapter Three

The following morning, Cupid decided to check out the other reports of mischief Santa had reported to him. The first being Santa's closet. Though Clara had cleaned and tidied up the area, Cupid felt he needed to follow all trails of "monkey business" Santa had reported.

Clara provided Cupid with the bag of ripped and cut apparel. Cupid dumped it onto the floor, with Clara's permission, of course, to see the prank's output. If one didn't know what the original item was, they might never have known. Santa's suit was a pile of red velvet and white fur confetti.

Cupid's first thought was there must have been great hate behind such a task, something he just hadn't seen in the tired little people of the village. Hate didn't seem to be in their blood, and if there were ill feelings toward Santa and Christmas in general, why now, after centuries of working together? It puzzled Cupid and just didn't add up.

"So sad to see such an heirloom in disrepair," Clara said as she watched Cupid spread and fan out the tatters of fabric.

"Indeed, Mrs. Kringle. It must have taken you months to make," he said sadly.

"Oh dear, it was not me that made the suit, it was Chris's mother who lovingly created the iconic garment."

"That is a tragedy."

"It would have killed her to see it like this," she said, turning away to tend to something in the kitchen, though Cupid was quite sure her departure was more to hide the tears that he'd noticed welling in her eyes as she spoke.

Not seeing anything but sadness in the pile before him, he gathered the pieces and began to replace them in the bag. *So soft to the touch*, he thought as he did so. Must be silk velvet. What a travesty to see it like this—the very symbol of Santa and the goodness he exudes. Suddenly, he howled in pain. He opened his hand to find a small blade imbedded in the fleshy part of his palm. It sparkled blue and red in the light.

"Are you okay?" Clara inquired at the doorway.

"Yes, though I seem to have found a blade within the mess of fabric."

"Now that must smart," she said, coming closer.

"It does," he said as he pulled the knife out, with a small yelp.

She handed him the tea towel in her apron pocket and advised, "Hold that tight while I get my first aid kit."

He did as told and examined the instrument of his pain more closely. It was quite beautiful. Tiny blue and red gems adorned the wood of the handle. The blade was intricately etched in black tribal-looking decoration. Clara was back in a flash and bandaged him up nicely, and supplied him with a plateful of monkey bread to distract him from his pain.

"What is it?" she asked.

"I'm not sure. It looks like a little sickle—maybe it is the instrument used to destroy the cloth."

"Why would someone leave something so fine behind?" she asked, taking it from him and inspecting it herself.

"I suspect that was not their intent. More than likely a

surprise or scare was incurred in which the culprit dropped it in the pile of fabric. Realizing they might be caught, it was left behind in their fury to vacate." She handed it back to him.

"It's rather small to do all that damage," she said.

"True. It is small but deadly sharp. I imagine a pair of fiends in a flurry could have done the deed in the time allotted. Doesn't it look small for an elf? We know there were two criminals from the security footage, but they seemed rather short in stature for elves."

"I agree," she said, "though elves range greatly in size."

"I've noticed that, but even the smallest I've seen would have probably used something a bit bigger." She nodded in agreement.

"Thank you for the sweets and the first aid," he said as he turned back to the remains of the dwindled pile of red and white.

"Leave it. I'll take care of the rest."

"Are you sure?" he asked, grabbing the last piece of the pastry.

"Yes."

"Thank you."

"Keep us posted of your findings," she said as she put the last few remnants of cloth into the bag.

"I will, and thank you again," he said, pointing to his bandage.

She smiled as he turned and left.

Saddled up on a large moose, and holding a hand-drawn map, Cupid took off into the white landscape in search of the North Pole. Santa had drawn the map himself and told Cupid it had to be seen to be believed. Cupid wasn't sure what that meant, only that somehow the elves had done something to the iconic landmark.

What could they have done? he wondered. It's not like you can move the magnetic poles of the earth. Of course, he wasn't really sure WHAT the north pole was. Was it an actual post that marked the spot? Was it a region? Was there a big red X in the snow that informed one "you are here"? He didn't know, but he was going to find out.

Though it was mind-numbingly cold, his bum and the inside of his legs were warm from the behemoth of a beast he rode. Great puffs of steam blasted from its nostrils with each breath.

The map was little to no help for someone unfamiliar with a snow-covered terrain. Any landmarks that might be around were hidden under huge blankets of white powder, rendering them unremarkable. At one point, Cupid had the map upside down and checking the back for more information. The moose was annoyed at his uncertainty as it stood up to his belly in snow waiting for Cupid to decide which way to go.

"I'm sorry, Mr. Moose, but I haven't the foggiest idea which way to go. Do you see a giant rock anywhere? All I see are white lumps."

The moose snorted in response to the right. "That's a rock?" Cupid asked, though he wasn't really sure why he was depending on a moose for directions. The moose nodded impatiently.

"Okay. I'm game, as long as you know where you are going and how to get back, I'll follow your lead," Cupid answered.

The moose turned and started moving in the direction he had nodded. Cupid pocketed the map, pulled the collar of his coat tighter around his neck and said, "Lead on, noble moose." The moose shook its head in what Cupid could only construe as contempt.

They moved up the side of a large dune as the sun passed from behind a cloud, blinding Cupid for an instant. He squinted at the brightness until his eyes adjusted. What he saw was a forest of poles before him.

The hill looked like a giant pin cushion of red barber-style poles with a hand-painted, short, plank sign with the words "North Pole." Hundreds and hundreds of them littered the pristine white snow in every size imaginable.

If there was one "true" pole that was indeed the landmark, no one would even try to guess which one it might be.

Cupid dismounted the moose, sliding into the snow to his thighs. The moose pawed at the ground and found himself some frozen vegetation beneath to nibble on while Cupid walked among the sea of poles.

The picture he saw on Hilda's phone did not relay the vastness of the prank—it was mind-boggling to behold in person. If there were any evidence here, it was buried by many inches of snow. No footprints to see—nothing but sticks spiraled with red and white paint.

He waded into the rod-littered snow, admiring the time and effort it would have taken to complete such a task when he smacked his knee on something under the ice. He dug his way to the offending item to find a small shovel with a carved green handle. It took some hard wiggling to break it free of the frozen terrain, but it came loose and he wondered if maybe he'd found a piece of evidence.

Maybe on closer inspection of the carvings, he might find the owner of the shovel, but for now, he couldn't wait to get back on the warm moose and head back to the hotel where he was sure there would be hot cocoa and cookies waiting for him.

Back up on top of the moose and following the trail they had made to this spot, he turned his head to get one more glimpse of the sea of sticks and the immensity of it all before it was out of sight once more.

Whoever was behind this was clever, very motivated, and had a strange sense of humor, no doubt. He was sure this would not be the last great caper they'd see before the mystery was solved.

Cupid took the side door to the backstairs in hopes of grabbing some freshly-baked cookies on the way to his room, making a stop by another kitchen access for the lodge's guest services. The door had been ajar so he peeked his head in, hoping to ask one of the staff if he could have a cup of cocoa brought to his room to wash down his cookies, though no one was in the kitchen at the moment.

He thought it strange, but maybe they were just in the pantry or helping a customer. A frigid breeze blew past his face, making him shiver and hope that his parka would arrive tomorrow. Then he noted the back door was open.

Snow swirled in the wind, dusting the floor with flakes. What caught Cupid's attention, though, was what was under the snow. He moved forward when another gust of wind greeted him, slapping him in the face and making pots hanging behind him smack into one another, sounding primitive bell tones. He kneeled down to get a closer look.

They were muddy prints covered in straw or hay. He touched the dirty marks and brought his finger to his nose, hoping they weren't made of reindeer scat. Mixed with the straw was just that, reindeer poo. He made a disgusted face then wiped his fingers on his socks. As he did this, he noted the tracks stopped in front of a large burlap sack marked *Sugar*. Just to be on the safe side, he put a little sample of the sugar from the sack into a plastic baggie to look at later.

Nothing really strange about sugar and tracks to and from the barn, Cupid thought. Maybe they have extra storage in the barn. It would explain the marks and why the door was open. Despite his dismissal of it looking suspicious, he opted to write it down in his notebook.

He looked out the back door to see if there might be anyone there. Nobody was visible, but just over the sound of the wind, he heard voices.

He ventured out into the cold, keeping to the shadows and trying to control the chattering of his teeth. Just across the way in a pool of overhead light were fifteen to twenty elves in a circle. They kept their voices low and Cupid didn't dare get any closer without alerting them to his presence.

He stood and watched from a jutted corner of the building with the added obscurity from the darkness of an overhang. Though Cupid could not hear what was being said or who was in the circle, he got the impression they were hatching up some sort of plan.

With a murmur of agreement, the circle dispersed and scattered in all directions. He was quite sure his feet were frozen solid as he waited for the last of them to be out of sight before venturing around the lodge and coming in the front door like any other patron.

He hobbled to his room and actually remembered to duck as he entered. He tossed the soggy newspaper and the laptop at the foot of the bed before depositing the now frozen cookies on the nightstand. He jumped into a hot shower and defrosted himself. It was painful at first, but after a moment the heat seeped into his bones and his body finally started to relax and stop shivering.

He thought about what he'd seen near the barn and

whether or not he should have pushed his way closer. A good detective always took chances for the greater good, but this was his first case and he wanted to be careful and not go beyond his comfort zone until he had a little more experience under his belt.

With his skin a bright cherry red, he longed for some rest and headed to the bed. Checking his phone for messages and grabbing another cookie, he saw Santa had texted, asking if there was any progress.

Cupid thought to himself. He debated whether or not to tell Santa what he'd seen, but the call of the pillow that awaited him won out over his obligation to his client. After all, what had he really seen? A meeting. It might not have even been secret, for all Cupid knew.

He rubbed his forehead and immediately remembered all the hits it had taken today from the tiny doorways. That cinched it. What he'd seen could wait until morning. With that, Cupid turned out the lights and slept deep and sound.

Chapter Four

Opening his overnight packages of warmer clothes at the front desk, Cupid found the little village to be all abuzz. Elves were running around the streets carrying pumpkins. Cupid hadn't realized elves were so into Halloween, of course, there were a lot things about elves Cupid didn't know.

He smiled at their preparations, when he saw a little elf truck go by with a few hundred or more pumpkins. He made a comment to the elf behind the front desk who was arranging some small pumpkins on the counter from a box on the floor. "Such enthusiasm for Halloween. Will there be a Halloween dress-up party, too?"

She looked at him as if quite puzzled. "A dress-up party? Why? We only dress-up for Christmas."

Now it was Cupid who was puzzled. "So you just decorate for Halloween?"

Again, she was with the puzzled looked.

"The pumpkins," he said, as if trying to jar her thoughts.

She shook her head, not understanding his question.

"Do you celebrate Halloween?" he asked.

"No," she said, seemingly relieved by being able to

understand to what he was referring, but Cupid was even more puzzled.

"So you don't celebrate Halloween, yet everywhere I look, there are pumpkins. Here," he pointed to her arrangement, "on the street," he pointed out the window. It was then that he noticed just how many pumpkins there were. He went to the window.

Aside from truck load after truck load of pumpkins lined up on the street, there were orange squashes everywhere. Piles of them were scattered around. They lined the sidewalks and adorned every window.

He ran to the door and opened it, tripping over a crate of pumpkins next to several more boxes overflowing with them. When he turned to confront the elf he'd been talking to, he'd found she was gone.

He closed the door and went into the restaurant, noting the specials written on the blackboard in neon orange. "Pumpkin pancakes, pumpkin spice muffins, pumpkin waffles and pumpkin soufflé" were just a few listed. *What in the world is going on?* Cupid thought to himself as several elf men bumped into him heading in to eat. Inside the eatery, he found every table with one or three tiny pumpkins. They littered the circumference of the room and lined every window.

He followed an elf who seated him and took his order. He wrote some notes on his pad, but mostly he sat puzzling over hordes of pumpkins. He took a sip of his coffee finding it, too, had been flavored with pumpkin. It wasn't that it was not good, it just wasn't what his taste buds had expected and it threw him off a bit. His face must have looked like he'd sucked on a lemon since Santa looked at him strangely when he plopped down in the chair across from Cupid.

"Well, they've done it again," he said.

"They? What's been done?" Cupid said, stumbling over his words.

"What? This. Have you not noticed the pumpkins everywhere?"

"Well, yes, I have. What is up with that?"

"I think your detecting skills need some improvement," Santa said, shaking his head.

"You mean, this, this pumpkin stuff is not normal?"

"No, it's not normal. When have you ever seen a pumpkin in the arctic circle?"

"Never, but then I don't know what counts for normal up here, either, aside from candy canes, reindeer, presents, and elves. I assumed maybe they celebrated Halloween, but when I pressed the question with the desk clerk, she barely seemed to know what Halloween was at all."

"Elves don't celebrate anything but Christmas. As far as they know, there are no other holidays."

"Then why all the pumpkins?" Cupid asked.

Santa handed him the *New York Times*. The headlines read "Northern US is Pumpkin-less."

"I don't understand," Cupid said.

"The elves," Santa said in a hushed voice looking around, "they've gone and stolen all the pumpkins."

"How could that be? And why?"

"Isn't that why I hired YOU? To find out the why?"

Cupid shook his head, a little embarrassed. "And as for the *how*, we do deliver presents all over the world in one night, if you've been out of the loop for the last few centuries."

"I wonder if the meeting I observed last evening had anything to do with this caper?"

"You mean you had information about this and you didn't let me or Hilda know?"

"No. I mean, yes. Well, maybe. I'm not sure if what I saw

had anything to do with it. I couldn't get close enough to hear what they were talking about, but I did have the feeling they were planning something. I just never thought they'd be capable of something so HUGE."

"You're not really giving me much confidence in your detecting abilities, Cupid."

"I'm sorry, Santa. I promise, I won't let you down again."

"If we can't contain whatever is going on, I'm not sure what we're going to do. We're already grossly behind in manufacturing and now with all these crazy, nonsensical occurrences that have to be cleaned up, I don't know if Christmas is going to happen this year. Things around here usually work like a well-greased wheel. We've never had such a development—ever."

"We'll figure this out, Santa."

"I hope you're right, Cupid. I sure hope you're right."

Cupid felt bad about letting Santa down. He'd been really unprepared for this trip and it showed poorly on him. He should have warned Santa of the possibility of a plan being formulated. Sure, he didn't know for sure, but his gut had told him the elves were up to something, especially with the history of late.

He spent the better part of the day at the library looking over books of elven anatomy, biology and history, but none of it really gave him any insight on what might be causing this rash of strange behavior among them.

The elves themselves were cordial to him, but they were suspicious after Hilda had informed them he'd been investigating. He tried to talk with one of the older elves he'd heard was soon to celebrate his four hundredth birthday, but his memory was starting to fail him and he'd heard of Cupid's spying.

Needless to say, the pleasant conversation shed no light on the problem. Everyone he talked to was eager to please, quick to avail themselves, and always greeted him with a pleasant smile—not the attributes of such behavior.

To some extent, they seemed oblivious of the actions. It must have taken a great number of them to pull off such a caper as stealing most every pumpkin north of the thirty-seventh parallel. Obviously, some magic was involved, but there was still the *how* that bothered Cupid. Even the large elves couldn't hold more than two pumpkins and they didn't have wings like fairies or cherubs. He puzzled on that for a while when it hit him. The reindeer—they must have been involved somehow.

Sporting his new red snow pants, his bright pink parka, and topping the package off with his fedora, he proudly headed for the barn. He was toasty warm as he crunched through the snow, tipping his hat to a pretty blonde elven woman. As he approached the giant barn, he noted a strange thing peeping out of the snow.

It was a head with a tiny little purple hat. He thought it was a statue, for what in the world would stand stoically in the snow up to its neck without moving or trying to get out. When he investigated it further, the statue winked, startling Cupid.

"You're alive?" Cupid questioned.

"Of course. Don't be stupid," it replied.

"Are you an elf? Do you need help?"

"NO, and no. The name is Simon," it said.

Its tone was cross and at first, Cupid was going to just let the crabby thing be, but it, too, had piqued his interest.

"What are you?" Cupid finally mustered.

"A gnome, dummy. What are YOU? A fat old fairy?

Cupid was insulted. "NO. I'm Cupid."

"What's a cupid?" the vexing little man said.

"No. Cupid is my name. I'm a cherub," he responded.

There was no reply.

"I'm big around Valentine's Day. I shoot my arrow at people, unleashing love between couples that need that added extra push. I'm told I'm quite the matchmaker," Cupid explained, pointing to his bow and quiver filled with heart-adorned arrows flung over his shoulder.

An odd look came over Simon's face.

Cupid could only assume it was fear he saw. "I think you've misunderstood. I don't hurt people with my arrows…" He started to tell the strange stubby man, but instead changed his train of thought. "It doesn't matter. I'm not here in that capacity." The gnome stared straight ahead, refusing to make eye contact.

"I'm a private investigator," Cupid announced.

Not a peep came from Simon.

"Are you sure you're okay? Have you slipped into a hypothermic-induced coma?"

"If I had, would you go away?"

"No. I'd try to help."

"Well, I haven't, so don't. Instead, go away. You're very annoying."

"I'm annoying? Well, you're very crabby, Simon," Cupid said in a huff, leaving the little irritable gnome behind him as he grumbled something belligerent under his breath.

Cupid made his way to his room to mull over the evidence he had accumulated. He'd lifted a tiny partial fingerprint from the sickle following the instructions in his "How-to" book and was proud to have produced his first substantiation against the culprit or culprits.

He looked at the baggie he'd collected, labeled "sugar," but upon further analysis he found that though the substance was sweet, it was not sugar. Why would someone substitute the sugar for this substance and what was this sweet concoction? He hadn't a clue, but he felt confident something would give and set him on the path to solving this case. He owed it to Santa.

He made some notes on his pad and contemplated different scenarios, but nothing came to him. He'd have to maybe share his findings with Hilda. Maybe she could shed some light onto what he had uncovered.

Inside the stables was warm and cheery. There were hundreds of stalls that ran the length of the barn. The smallest, but nicest, barn was set aside for those reindeer chosen for Christmas Eve. Its inhabitants changed from year to year, based on who was the strongest and the fastest to pull the sleigh.

These eight prestigious reindeer were pampered and waited on by a number of dutiful elves. The other stables housed a long lineage of reindeer that dated back to the very first flight of the sleigh.

It was quite a sight to see and only a very few have ever wandered the Christmas stables of Santa. Cupid felt a sense of honor, being one of the chosen to explore their interiors at will. He did, however, expect there to be more activity, but most of the stalls were silent. No jingling of bells, no stomping or pawing, and no grunting or huffing.

Cupid peered into one of the stalls to see a reindeer bedded down in the corner on a great pile of hay. The next stall was the same. In fact, not one of the stalls that Cupid looked in contained a reindeer that was awake.

Not only were the reindeer asleep, but the elves were scattered around the barn sleeping as well. Some sat up back to back, some were in the stalls with the reindeer. Wherever there was an elf, there, too, was a plate of bright red, gold, green, and white crumbs and frosting from what Cupid was quite sure were the remnants of cookies.

How strange. Are reindeer nocturnal? He didn't think so, but it was something he'd better check. Maybe once chosen, the reindeer were put on a night schedule to increase their stamina. *But why are all the elves asleep, too?* he wondered. More likely, they were tired from an evening of traveling.

That cinched it. The reindeer had been used the night before to bring all the pumpkins from the south to the north. Each must have pulled a cart or sleigh of its own and from the looks of it, they were exhausted from their travels. The elves must be bushed from all the antics, too.

He made his way to the sleigh closest to him. Upon inspection, he found orange goo and scuffs on the floor and interior of the cargo area. Pulling a piece of paper from his notebook, he used it to scrape and scoop up some orange evidence into a small baggie. He smelled it as he did so and tasted the remains on the paper....*definitely pumpkin*, he thought to himself.

It felt good to have the *how* established, but it was still the *why* that confused him. As far as he had gathered from his interviews and his research, malevolence didn't fit the profile of elves. Maybe he should take another look at the north poles and the polar bears for clues.

He would have normally had an elf hitch a couple of reindeer to a sleigh for his trip out to detect what he could, but with all the napping inhabitants of the barn, he opted to saddle a moose instead.

Chapter Five

The trip to the polar bears and their lagoon was much more pleasant this time with more appropriate attire. The lack of shivers allowed Cupid to take in the beauty around him. Though starkly populated and sparsely vegetated, the scenery was magnificent.

The bells on the moose's harness seemed to make a nice companion for the setting. Cupid reminisced on many a sleigh ride he was privy to that were the beginning of some happy, long-lasting relationships.

Ahead, he spied a familiar looking snowmobile parked. Had Hilda had the same idea? He hoped not. He'd already had more run-ins with her than he'd like. She did not seem to appreciate his presence or his help. If she was here, she'd just have to live with it. He'd made a promise to Santa and he aimed to fulfill it.

On foot, it was slow moving in the deep snow. Thankfully, he was able to use the tracks the snowmobile owner had made. Based on their size, there was no guessing as to who they belonged to. It had to be Hilda as he suspected. He could see her in the distance as he passed over a berm.

He felt she was terribly close to the polar bears considering they were not known for their friendliness. She was looking at a polar bear and when it spied him coming, it reared up on its back legs, standing like a man. Hilda turned to see what had caught the bear's attention.

Cupid was close enough to see her dissatisfied expression, but with her back turned toward the bear, she didn't see it drop onto four paws and take off into a full-out run toward her.

Cupid wasted no time pulling an arrow from the quiver and loading his bow. It wouldn't kill the bear, but it would hopefully change its hunger to feed to a need for love. The look on Hilda's face changed from disapproving to downright fear as he took aim.

The arrow soared through the air, piercing the bear in the shoulder and exploding into a shower of red glitter. It stopped the bear in its track and sent it veering to the left where a female bear frolicked in the icy water.

For the first time since he met Hilda, she was speechless and friendly.

"Nice shooting," she finally said.

"Thanks. I haven't missed a target in nearly five hundred years, though it's not usually used defensively," he joked.

"Well, I, for one, am grateful for that," she said, eyeing the two bears now chasing one another on the ice like two cubs.

"You out here, like me, for a second look to see if we missed anything?"

"Yup. Have anything to report on your end?" she asked.

"Only that I'm pretty sure the elves used the reindeer for transporting the pumpkins here."

"Oh?"

"Almost every stall in the stables is housing a sleepy reindeer right now."

"Hmm. Well, it's a lead if nothing else."

"That's my thought. It's strange, though, there's no sign of the elves attempting to conceal their hand in the act. I mean, their footprints are all over the crime scenes."

"True."

"Wouldn't you think they'd be more discreet since they tend to be so organized and precise on the whole?"

"One might think so," she pondered.

"And what exactly could they be gaining by carrying out these pranks?"

"Nothing I can see as yet."

"Me either. It just doesn't add up," he said as they headed back to their vehicles. It was silent for a while when Cupid said, "I met my first gnome today."

"Interesting critters," she noted.

"I don't know about interesting, but certainly crabby."

"Yes, they are."

"Why, do you suppose?"

"Would you be a cheerful fellow standing around all day doing nothing?"

"Probably not. Is that their sole purpose in life?"

"It would seem so, at least during the day. Gnome's are mostly known for their gardening and not much else, as far as I can tell. How does one such as yourself become a private investigator? And why, when you already have a career?"

"I like helping people, and well, matchmaking, as great as it is, can get a little tasking after a few hundred years. Let's face it, an old man in a diaper just doesn't appeal to the masses as a symbol of love. I have trainees now that do the bulk of the work. I only take on the hard-core cases when they pop up now and again. Besides, I wanted to mix things up a bit—things were getting stale."

She said, "The majority of being a detective is spying on spouses that are suspected of cheating. Doesn't that kind of go against your first career?"

"One might think that. It's true. But it gives me the opportunity to see the other side of the coin, so to speak. Knowing the ins and outs of both sides helps in recognizing what breaks up couples. My thought is I can hopefully help them mend their fences and get them back on the path to finding their way back into each other's arms."

"That's a very romantic notion. How's it working out for you?" she asked.

"Not so great at the moment, since I'm on a case about misbehaving elves."

Hilda laughed in agreement. "Your first case?"

"Yup."

"Well, it's certainly a doozy. If you can pull this off then I have no doubt you'll be an excellent P.I."

"Thanks. That means a lot coming from someone in your profession."

"You're welcome," she smiled as they arrived at the sleigh.

"Any information you can give me about elves?" he asked.

"Hmm. Well, like trolls, they've been around forever. They obviously like to make things from cookies, toys, cleaning, and shoemaking—seems to make them happy. They range in sizes, live in all kinds of climates all over the world. And they LOVE sweets."

"That I've noticed. I haven't had many vegetables since I've been here, aside from the pumpkins," Cupid noted.

"If it weren't for the Kringle's visitors like you and my crew of trolls, there would be no vegetables at all."

"I'm guessing all that sugar is what makes them hyperactive."

"Don't know, but for as much as they eat, they never seem to get very fat."

"Wish I could say the same," Cupid said, patting his belly. Hilda giggled.

"I hear ya," she said. Cupid figured trolls were not known for their svelte lean bodies, though he didn't feel Hilda was overweight my any means—probably just right for a troll. Course, he'd only known a few trolls from his past. She was by far more trim than any other he'd seen.

"I have found some evidence I'd like to share with you," Cupid said, reaching into his pocket. "Maybe you can shed some light on them."

He held up a baggie with an orange substance. "This I believe is pumpkin flesh that I found in one of the sleighs in the stable. I think it tells us that the reindeer and extra sleighs were indeed used to confiscate the hordes of pumpkins, but I dare say, I haven't a clue as to *why* they would do such a thing."

Hilda examined the contents in the baggie and opened it to confirm the smell of pumpkin it exuded. She concurred what he had suspected to be true. "Makes sense magic was involved. They aren't big enough and there aren't enough of them to have done this on foot by themselves."

"Exactly."

"This is a fingerprint I attained off this tiny sickle I found in the shreds of Santa's suit," he said, handing Hilda two plastic bags. "The problem is, I don't have access to a fingerprint database, especially for the magical beings, though I think that if we are able to solve these crimes, I might be allowed access to such information in the future, by the council. Would you be willing to run the print for me in the interim?"

"Sure. And good work," she said with a hint of a smile. "You said you found this sickle in the remnants bag?"

"Yes, quite by accident. While plunging through the pile I grasped the blade, embedding it in my palm."

"Ouch, that must have smarted."

"It did, but Mrs. Kringle was quick to bandage me up."

"Isn't she the nicest lady?"

"Yes."

"I'll definitely run this through the database, but I will tell you, don't hold your breath. The data within is only for those magical beings who have been processed for some kind of crime."

"Of course, but if we're lucky it might produce something."

"You bet."

"And my last bit of evidence is this," he said, handing her a Ziploc of the white substance labeled "Sugar."

"Sugar? How is that evidence?" she asked.

"It's probably nothing. I found this substance in a sack in the hotel kitchen. Its crystals aren't as big as regular sugar, which is what I assumed would be in the bag. I thought maybe it was a finer type, made for icings and such, but taste it. It's sweeter than what I think of as sugar."

She examined it and then licked her pinkie and dipped it into the substance, then dabbed a bit of it on her tongue. "Hmm. You're right, so there's a bag of some kind of substitute sugar?"

"I found tiny muddy footprints that led from the barn to the kitchen. I probably wouldn't have noticed it at all if the back door to the kitchen hadn't been opened."

"And?"

"It could be nothing, but something strikes me as odd about it. We believe that the instigators of these hoaxes are very small. I mean, look at the knife."

She did, being careful not to rip the bag, but by the expression on her face, he could see she wasn't connecting the dots. "Elves are small. I don't see where you're going with this."

"You are correct. Elves are small and come in a variety of sizes, but the footprints I saw"—(he showed her a picture he'd taken on his phone)—"and the blade are exceptionally small. Smaller than the smallest elf I've seen thus far would use."

"Maybe it was a toy from their childhood."

"What parent in their right mind would give a small child, elf or no, a razor-sharp toy?" he stated. She raised her eyebrows, telling him that she understood his range of thought.

"I think we are looking for one or multiple very small elves with chips on their shoulders."

"But elves don't roll that way. I've never seen an elf in any kind of rage. Sure, they get frustrated, but even then I wouldn't say they really are mad."

"And that's been my finding, too. Whatever is going on is very unlike elves. I mean, look around you. Is it normal for the elves to be passed out sleeping everywhere you look?"

"You've got me there. In all my time here in the Great North, I think I've only seen one or two elves snoozing or napping, and they were ancient old. But then again, they stole all the pumpkins in the northern United States. That certainly would make me tired."

"No doubt, but elves are different. They were made for this kind of stuff, so to speak. My research shows that elves sleep very little and that is why they are so perfect for what they do. Who else could make toys for every child in the world in just a year's time? No one I know, magical or not," he pressed.

"So what are you saying? That the criminals are not elves?"

"It's possible, don't you think?"

She squinted at the comment, as if not totally agreeing with his deductions.

"Why would these creatures, whatever you think they might be, use the elves to do their bidding?"

"That IS the question. WHY indeed?"

"Well, I'll run the print through the database and have my

lab confirm the substances you've found. I'll also see if anyone has come across a sickle like this on my team."

"Great. Oh, and I'm not sure if there are any prints on it, but here's a little shovel I found up in the 'field of poles.' Smacked my knee on it and pulled it up not knowing what it was, so I've probably smudged any evidence that might have been on it."

"Okay. You do seem to find your evidence rather painfully," she joked.

"I do," he agreed, chuckling and rubbing the bandaged palm of his hand.

"I better get back to work," she said, mounting her snowmobile.

He got into the sleigh and said, "It's been a pleasure, Ms. Rocke. Thank you for your input and your pleasant company."

Her glacier-blue eyes sparkled at the compliment and suddenly a blush of color and an ear-to-ear smile emerged on her lips. "Thank YOU, for saving my life. I'd have been a pile of polar bear chow if it hadn't been for you and your excellent marksmanship."

He smiled at her remark and saw a beauty in her he'd not seen before. This less aggressive side of her gave her a charm of loveliness that made his heart skip a beat and blush a bit himself.

"Goodbye. Hope to see you soon."

"You will. It's a small town," she said, starting the deafening engine of the snowmobile. She waved as she headed back to town.

He followed her lead in the sleigh at a more leisurely pace.

He thought about her as he listened to the bells chiming with every footfall from the moose. In all his years, he'd never before had the flutter he felt in his heart now. How odd. In his profession, he'd never found love for himself. Maybe he'd never really had time. He was always working and always traveling with no time to settle down and have a love of his own.

He'd never really missed it, but now for some reason that seemed kind of sad to him. Had he missed out on something he'd been giving to all of humanity from the beginning of time and lost his chance at a happily ever after? "Maybe...but then again, maybe not," he said out loud to no one, with a grin.

Despite attempts by Santa, Cupid, and the Arctic Troll Patrol at returning the pumpkins back to the southern lands, Halloween was a mess. The pumpkins had frozen in the north and when they brought them back to the pumpkin patches all over the northern states of the U.S. and Canada, they were a gooey mess.

Pumpkins didn't freeze well and they were useless for jack-o'-lanterns—too soggy to cut. Newspapers suggested elaborate conspiracy theories as to why mushy squashes were distributed everywhere in place of the beacons of Halloween that had been stolen. It was a shamble in every aspect.

Santa and the trolls were exhausted as were the reindeer, who were used to only one overnight trip a year but now already had two under their harness and they hadn't even reached December.

Over the next few weeks, Santa and Clara tried to encourage the elves back to their duties, and though the tiny people took their posts, very little production was achieved. They seemed to have no focus whatsoever. The couple took to running production themselves as best they could. Hilda, her crew, and Cupid tried to help out between interviewing elves. Having no experience in the factory and all its machines, very little was achieved.

Hilda put in a call for help to her kin back in Iceland to come lend a hand, but as she had informed the Kringles and Cupid, trolls were not known for their quickness. She hoped they'd make it in time, but it was a shot in the dark at best.

Thanksgiving was fast approaching and Cupid and the ATL were no closer to solving the mystery of the elves than they were at Halloween. Cupid sent for his cherubs, leaving a skeleton crew to run the business of love, but he soon found that they were ill-equipped at anything mechanical. They spent most of their time playing with the emotions of the elves instead of actually working and two days before Thanksgiving, he sent them away. They were causing far more chaos than the elves were.

While on a shift in the factory, Cupid had left his post for a bathroom break. On his way back, he stumbled upon a pow-wow of elves in a circle in a room. The door had not shut all the way and Cupid was able to stand beside it and hear the hushed voices speaking.

"Our pumpkin plan went so well, we're going to ramp up the next," a voice from within the center of the circle said. The culprit could not be seen. The elves giggled with delight at this statement. "The humans will never expect our foul plot."

Foul plot? Cupid wondered.

"Tiny, you are in charge of gearing up the reindeer. Red, you're in charge of orchestrating take offs and landings. Enid, you're going to be in charge of unloading the cargo and handing off available reindeer back into the queue for the next destination. Blu, your team is in charge of clean up—getting the reindeer back into their stalls, fed, and watered. Are we clear?"

A hushed flurry of excited ayes and yeses came from the bunch.

"Make sure you get your paperwork form, Shortie, before you leave. Okay? Good. Project Foul is underway. Oh, and don't forget to take a cookie. I baked them fresh this morning," the unseen leader encouraged.

I better get out of her before I'm seen, Cupid thought to himself, and he took off like the wind texting Santa and Hilda for a meeting.

Chapter Six

"What is it?" Santa urged Cupid. "I've got a lot of work to do and not enough time to do it." Hilda walked in just as Clara was setting down a plate of delicious looking cookies.

"I've overheard another plot the elves are putting together," Cupid said happily.

"Another one?" Clara said, yawning and taking a sip of coffee. "I wish I had their energy," she added. "Think how many toys I could make if I had a fraction of their stamina."

"Think how many toys THEY could make if they'd get back to doing their jobs," Santa said, yawning himself.

"You two need some sleep," Hilda suggested.

"If only we could," Santa said, patting his wife's hand in appreciation of her help.

"So what is this plot you've uncovered?" Santa asked.

"I'm not sure. I just know that tonight, they're using the reindeer again for something they're calling the 'Foul Project.' They were distributing instructions to one another as to what their responsibilities are to be."

"Foul project. That doesn't sound like something an elf would be involved in. They're happy, kind little people," Clara offered.

"Nothing about this whole crisis makes sense, dear," Santa said. "Elves are workers. They love to work, yet I can't get a one to work."

"It's true. They seem aimless and confused, wandering around town doing nothing in particular but not standing still either," Hilda added.

"I know. I can't explain it, but I will get to the bottom of this. In the meantime, if we can hamper their plans, maybe it will throw them off their game and shed some light on who the ring leader is and why they're acting so odd," Cupid said.

"I think he's right," Hilda said. This seemed to shock Santa, but he listened to her explanation. "I say we follow them a bit see if we can get any intel before we disrupt their plan. The more of the plan that we uncover before they discover we're on to them, might just give us the edge we need to solve this mystery."

"Okay. If Hilda's in, then you two go for it. Clara and I will try and get some production out while you go on your stake out. We'll meet up later and you can give us an update."

"Sounds good," Cupid said. Clara and Santa took their leave.

"I'll meet you in the stables after dark," Hilda said.

"I'll try and see if I can get my hands on one of those flyers I saw them handing out. Maybe someone has set it down and forgotten about it. Might give us a clue."

"Good thinking. I'll also get some food for our stakeout."

"Perfect," Cupid agreed and they went their separate ways.

Though Cupid was able to get an abandoned instruction sheet, it was written in elfish shorthand and completely unreadable to him. When he met up with Hilda in an empty stall, he showed it to her. She could not decipher the scribble either, but she thought that one of the symbols referred to a bird or flying craft. She wasn't sure.

It was nice to have a companion, though they couldn't really speak for fear of someone hearing them. They were well-equipped with plenty of food and a warm place to hide. They were there not more than thirty minutes before they had company. Several elves were about, moving hesitant reindeer here and there. But it wasn't until two elves walked by having a conversation that something dawned on Cupid.

"I hate them," one elf said.

"Why?" the other asked.

"They're ugly things."

"They're different, but I don't know if I'd say they're ugly."

"Well, I think they're ugly. I mean they've got that weird red skin on their heads and fleshy thing on their necks—what's up with that?"

"I don't know, I guess the girls like it."

"Well, then, the girls are weird."

"Fine, but ALL girls are weird, aren't they?" one said.

The other laughed. "You got me there."

"Hey, I heard that they're so dumb that they'll drown in a rain storm from staring up at the sky."

"That's a wives' tale."

"It is not."

"Is, too. Don't be a goof."

"I'm not, that's what I heard."

"Well, you heard wrong. I heard that turkeys are quite smart and can be nice pets."

"Gross, I'd never have one as a pet. Pets should always be smaller than their owner," one said.

"You could ride it like people ride ostriches. We could have turkey races. That would be cool," he heard one say as they left the building.

"Oh my God. It's not a 'foul' project, it's a 'fowl' project," Cupid said in a whisper.

"They're going to steal all the turkeys for Thanksgiving," Hilda retorted.

"Yes, and the pumpkins were just a test to see if they could do it."

"We've got to tell the Kringles."

"Right," she said, "you go get them and I'll round up the ATP, and we'll put a stop to this 'Fowl Project.'"

"Meet you back here in ten minutes," he said.

"Roger that," she confirmed.

It was just a matter of minutes between telling the Kringles about the plan, to executing the demise of it. Santa stood before the first of the prepped reindeer as the elves approached. Like a stack of dominos, the elves halted at the sight of him, running into one another and gasping at the surprise of it all.

It reminded Cupid of a line of ants following a path only to have a leaf fall onto it and causing a brief panic among ranks when they didn't know where to go. When a good number of them were present and frantic with confusion, Santa made a speech.

"My dear elves. It has come to my attention that some sort of turkey-napping plan has been hatched. I don't know why or what has caused this, this, unelven-like behavior, but I'd like to have these pranks put to an end. If I have somehow offended you," he said to a barrage of *no* from the elven audience.

"Or you think I don't appreciate your services," disconcerted chatter scattered among them. "Please come speak to me and let us hash out these differences, but let's not take our squabbles beyond our little town or make our human friends to the south suffer for our problems. Drop your burlap sacks, go back to the warmth of your beds and forget this shenanigan for good."

Cupid watched as the elves dropped their bags and left. Though they seemed agitated, it didn't seem to be directed at Santa or anyone else. It appeared to be more like unspent energy looking for a vent. There was no argument or fallout from Santa's speech. It was the strangest thing.

The next day, Santa expected to have a swarm of elves at his door and he had prepared himself by organizing a backup staff to help with the surplus by enlisting Cupid, Hilda, and Clara, but there was none. No one came to see him to voice their issues and not a soul came into work, which was par for the course lately. It dumbfounded Santa and his recruits. If they had no bone to pick with Santa, why not come to work?

Cupid said to Hilda, "It's as if they've been brain-washed. They don't seem to grasp what's happening, they just do as their leader says."

"Up until mid-October that leader was Santa, who is it now? And why has it changed?"

"I don't have a clue," Cupid admitted as he watched Clara console a sad and anxious Santa.

"Well, now that Santa confronted the elves, maybe the pranks will come to an end."

"One can only hope, but I wouldn't hold my breath if I were you."

Hilda nodded in agreement.

"Hilda, is there any new information on the items I gave you?" Cupid asked.

"Items?" Santa queried.

"None as of yet. We're still processing them," Hilda informed Cupid.

"I gave Hilda some evidence I have gathered—a print I lifted off the sickle and pumpkin confirming the reindeer and sleighs had been used to transport the pumpkins, among others."

"Keep it up. I can't thank you enough for helping avert what could have been a terrible end to yet another holiday. I've been getting hourly texts from the council who is in an uproar about the Halloween disaster. If the 'Fowl Project' had happened, I fear I might have lost my job and then there would definitely not be a Christmas, though at the rate of things, I'm not sure it's going to happen either way."

"Don't say that," Hilda said.

"I'm sorry, Hilda, but it's the truth. Normally at Thanksgiving, we are done with production and are in the wrapping/packing phase, but we're barely at 50 percent of production completion and I don't see how the four of us can keep up this pace for too much longer without a lot of help."

"I'm sorry the cherubs weren't a help, Santa," Cupid admitted.

"It's not your fault; you tried to help. It's just not in a young cherub's DNA to work like an elf."

"You'd think there'd be some other option among all the magical beings in the world," Clara voiced.

"Most magical creatures are not gifted with the work ethic and dedication of an elf."

"We'll just do our best. That's all we can do, dear."

"I suppose you're right, Clara...I just hate disappointing the children."

"I know, dear. I know."

Santa and Clara headed back to the production line, leaving Hilda and Cupid there to digest the direness of the situation.

"I wish there was something we could do."

"You're doing it, Hilda," Cupid said.

"I am?"

"Yes. You're working hard at apprehending the culprit, as am I. We're both working side by side with the Kringles in our spare time to help, and you've called in your kin to help."

"Lot of good that's done."

"But you did it. It's not like my idea of bringing in the cherubs did much good, but we've both tried. Right? And that's what matters at the end of the day."

"What about all those children who will go without gifts this Christmas?"

"I know. It bothers me, too, but unless you have an idea you haven't voiced yet, I don't see what else we can do."

"Maybe there is, or at least, there might be something you can do," Hilda said with a glint in her pretty blue eyes.

Cupid stood stunned and wondered what she had up her sleeve.

Chapter Seven

It wasn't long after the aversion of the "Fowl Project" that there was dissension among the reindeer. Cupid caught wind of some rumors that the Kringles and the ATP had been summoned to the stables.

When Cupid arrived, a large number of reindeer were snorting and grunting something awful. They pawed at the sod and hay, splaying it at an angle behind them. The head bull even reared up when an elf tried to pull in the reins.

"What is going on?" Santa queried the head stable elf. "Why are they so unhappy?"

The elf made no sign of knowing how to answer Santa's questions so Cupid stepped forward. "Maybe I can help?" he offered.

"Not unless you speak reindeer," Santa retorted.

"Actually, I might be able to help in that area. Love is not just for humans but animals, too. I have, in my travels, had to decipher many languages and species. In fact, this one time I had—" Cupid said, but Santa cut him off.

"Now's not the time for your stories, Cupid. If you can talk with them then do so—now."

"It's not so much as talking," Cupid offered before getting stopped by an irritated Santa.

Santa rubbed his face starting at his forehead and ending by scratching is chin under the thick white beard. "Can we just get on with it?"

"Right." Cupid approached the bull and nodded to him. He made some grunts and snorts which were met with the same from his adversary. They both pawed at the ground and nodded their heads to one another. After a few minutes of this, Cupid emerged from his consult with the head bull and turned to Santa.

"Well?" Santa said anxiously.

"They're upset by the elves' use of them and your lack of controlling the elves. They refuse to work for either at this point until they see fit."

"They're striking?" Santa asked.

"It would seem so."

"Swell. As if things aren't bad enough with production, now I have no delivering mechanism in place." Santa reached for his Panama hat he'd taken to wearing with the demise of his wardrobe and threw it on the ground in frustration.

The stable elves all gasped at his act and congregated outside. The reindeer snorted, shaking their heads, making their racks of antlers look more like weapons as they moseyed to their stalls, occasionally voicing their opinions to one another as they came in contact.

Cupid snatched the hat from the ground before it could be stepped on anymore. "It's a sad state of affairs," Hilda said.

"I can't imagine what he must be feeling," Cupid replied.

"I feel sorry for the Kringles. They're trying so hard to keep it together and nothing seems to be going their way."

"I know," Cupid said, leading Hilda out of the stables, then holding the large wooden door open for her as she exited.

"So much disappointment—for all," Hilda said, but Cupid didn't hear what she said, he was busy looking at the similar gathering of elves he saw the night before the pumpkins were stolen. He wasn't going to make the same mistake as last time and not confront them. He felt he had let Santa down that night by not getting closer to see what they were up to. But what to do?

Should he try to get close and see what the plan was, or should he bombard them by taking them off guard in hopes of getting a glimpse of the leader in the middle of the group? He decided the latter.

"I'm sorry, Hilda, please excuse me," he politely said then took off like one of his arrows of love to the assembly of elves.

Cupid had wings and speed, but it was no match for the elves. He felt he ran into a flock of sea gulls as they scattered so swiftly, it seemed somehow planned. Again, the only glimpse of the leader he got was a tiny shadow and a bright green hat.

Hilda came to his side. "Were you able to spy who was at the center?" she asked as if she knew what he'd planned.

"No. Only a hat and the shadow of a tiny person—lot of good that does us. They're all little. They all wear hats. Now if it had been bright pink or yellow, but no. Green. All of them wear either green or red hats and who is to say they don't change the color daily."

"Don't beat yourself up. We're in the same boat, at least you took the initiative to try and get a peek at the leader."

"Still we're no closer to solving this crazy case than we were weeks ago," he was frustrated by it all. He couldn't even look her in the face, so he headed back to the hotel to go over his notes once again and see if he'd missed something.

The following day, the little North Pole city was flooded with a barrage of fairies, dwarfs, imps, leprechauns, ogres, pixies, sprites, a great deal of witches and druids, and even those on the counsel showed, including Father Time, Mother Nature, the Easter bunny, the tooth fairy, as well as others. Cupid smiled at the sight of them when Hilda came up behind him, tapping him on the shoulder and smiling.

"You did good," Hilda said.

"It was your idea to call the council. I just hope they can help and not cause more of a problem."

Santa came out slipping on his robe for extra warmth in the snow. "What is this?" he asked.

Father Time stepped forward. "We're here to help. Cupid informed us just how dire things have become and we're here to do what we can to get what needs to be done."

"You mean you're willing to work on the production line in lieu of the elves?"

"Exactly. We may be a sad second to the elves' dexterity and expertise, but if a group of magical beings cannot be of some help, then that's not saying a whole lot about magic. Chris and Clara, you have always had our backs when things went wrong in our circles. It's time for us to show you just how much that's meant to us over the eons. Plus, we don't want to see the children go without."

"I can't tell you how much this means to us," Santa said, putting an arm around Clara. His eyes welled up at the generosity they'd poured upon the community. "Thank you so much."

They cheered and tossed magical dust into the air, littering the sky with glittery elements and fireworks.

"Okay then," Santa said with a smile and clapping his hands together, "let's get you started. Make a line here," he pointed and made a mark in the snow with his galoshes.

"After a few questions, we'll assign you a task that we think might accentuate your talents."

There was a murmur of voices, and one by one, each person was commissioned to an area. Cupid hadn't seen such a smile on Santa's face since he had arrived. He and Hilda had done a good thing.

Having been cleared of production duty, Clara was able to make progress on a new suit for Santa. It wasn't the exquisite antique that had been made by Chris's mother so long ago, but it did have some features she thought Chris might find handy during his trek across the skies.

It was a deep burgundy red velvet, silky soft, and lined with the finest fur donated by the beavers, and was much the same classic design as the previous, but with extra pockets for new-age necessities like his cell phone and tablet. She was diligent in her work and in no time at all, the task was done and ready to present to her husband. She had plenty of extra fabric for repairs and even cut out an extra pattern for a spare that she stored in an undisclosed location so as to not reprise the fate of the last suit.

Santa was pleased as punch and dropped his Bermuda shorts right there in order to wear his new warm pants. He noted to Clara in doing so, "Burn those. I don't ever want to see them again," Chris said, referring to the pants he discarded. Clara laughed.

"But I'll miss seeing those skinny little legs on a daily basis."

He laughed and twirled her around the room, giving her kiss after kiss and showing his immense appreciation of her efforts.

"It's not the one your mother made, but it'll do."

"It's perfect. I'll miss the other only due to the nostalgia behind its history, but THIS is made by YOU and I couldn't be happier and prouder to be wearing it."

He twirled her around once more before grabbing a brownie with a huge grin and then heading back to the production line where they were actually making a little headway with the help that had shown up. She prayed things would move forward and that the tribulations and vexing of the past months would cease. *One could only hope*, she thought with a sigh and smile.

Chapter Eight

While sitting at the tiny table in the cafe at the hotel sifting through his notes, Cupid spied Santa strolling in. Cheers and claps were had by all those awake, including Cupid. It was good to see Santa with an ear-to-ear smile, sporting his new duds.

"Good to see you in your new suit. It looks hip," Cupid complimented.

"I love it. I've never been so happy to wear normal pants in my life," Santa confessed.

"Well, technically, red velvet fur-trimmed trousers with embroidered holly suspenders is not what most would call 'normal,'" Cupid said as Santa sat at the table, summoning one of the waitresses with a nod and a wave of his hand.

"This coming from a man who wears pink long underwear under a trench coat on a 'normal' day."

"Touché," Cupid admitted. Santa ordered a cup of cocoa and gingerbread cookies.

"How are things going?" Cupid asked.

"Great. Production has increased 200 percent since the arrival of our magical friends."

"Then Christmas is saved?" Cupid hoped.

"I wouldn't jump to that conclusion, but it's a big push in

the right direction. Our biggest obstacle now is if we do meet production quotas AND get everything packed and wrapped, we have no way of delivering with the reindeer on strike."

"Hmm. I'm sure we can come up with something. Maybe I could talk to Dasher again, see if the reindeer have rethought things through."

"You could, but I doubt it will make a difference. Reindeer can be quite stubborn when they want to be," Santa said, sipping at his hot chocolate.

"Hmm. We could talk to the fairy folk and the witches, maybe they can help with delivery and or have some suggestions in how we can accomplish our goals."

"Can't hurt to try, though I hate to ask any more of them. They've all been so understanding and supportive, I'd hate to overstep my ground with them."

"It's not forever. It's just until we get this craziness solved and get things back to the way they were."

"Any new developments in that arena?" Santa said, waving to the waitress elf for a refill.

"No. I was going through my notes when you came in, trying to see if I missed anything," Cupid answered, noting Hilda entering the room. "But maybe Ms. Rocke has some test results back," he said, nodding to her to join them when they made eye contact.

"Hilda. Morning," Santa said as he also thanked the waitress.

"Santa. I see you've got your suit. Looks good."

"Thanks. Couldn't be happier to have it. Asked Clara to burn those Bermuda shorts."

Cupid and Hilda chuckled in stereo.

"Do you have any news for us?" Cupid asked anxiously, noticing her cheerful mood.

"I do. Though not all of it is definitive," Hilda said much to Santa's disappointment.

"Fingerprints?" Cupid asked excitedly.

"Yes, there was a hit...but with it being a partial and smudged a bit, it's not conclusive. However, there was a tiny bit of blood found on the sickle which at first I dismissed because I thought it was yours," she said to Cupid, "but as it turns out, it wasn't."

"Were you able to identify the culprit?"

"No. It was compromised, but what we could find was that it was gnomish."

"Gnomish blood? Not elven?"

"Definitely gnomish."

"Well, that's something. There's only three gnomes I know of here," Santa interjected.

"True, but with it being compromised, it's circumstantial at best."

"It would make sense, though, given the height of the ringmaster I've not been able to identify," Cupid said. "And the other tiny item I found was a shovel in the 'field of poles,' both are garden tools."

"Again, not solid evidence without fingerprints to place one of them there, certainly not enough to charge one with," Hilda said.

"But enough to bring the three of them in and question them."

"Definitely," Hilda affirmed.

"Good. Well, that's something," Santa added.

"Any other info?" Cupid asked.

"Yes, but I don't see how it's very helpful," Hilda answered.

"What's that?"

"The white substance labeled 'sugar' is sugar, but sugar substitute."

"I see. No crime there. I mean, plenty of people use sugar substitute."

"Wait a minute...what are you talking about?" Santa asked.

"A dead end, I suppose. I found sugar substitute in the kitchen here in a bag marked sugar. The only reason I grabbed a sample was because there were tiny footprints that came from outside and stopped at the sugar bag."

"So you're saying the elves have been cooking with sugar substitute?" Santa asked in alarm.

"I believe so. Why do you seem so concerned?"

"Because sugar substitute is like alcohol to an elf. It would make them prone to do things they wouldn't normally do," Santa proclaimed.

"I didn't know that," Hilda exclaimed.

"It's something the elves don't like to talk about. It's embarrassing to them," Santa whispered.

"Well, that would explain some things," Cupid said.

"Indeed. If someone swapped out the sugar for a substitute, knowing the results, they would be able to manipulate them into doing their bidding."

"But if the gnomes are involved, why would they do such a thing? I don't see a motive here."

"That, Cupid, is your department, but I think the two of you should bring in the gnome brothers and find out if they are involved, and why," Santa suggested.

Cupid and Hilda wasted no time bringing in Simon, Hermon, and Norman. It was Cupid's first time questioning accused assailants but thankfully, Hilda was a pro. The three of them sat on one side of the table while Cupid and Hilda sat on the other side. Cupid was armed with his notepad, and Hilda with a file folder of the results from the evidence collected by Cupid and a tape recorder which she switched on.

"It is November 10, 2018, 10:45 a.m. Sergeant Rocke here aided by Cupid in the questioning of the gnome brothers. Will you please state your names for the record," Hilda prompted.

"Simon."

"Hermon."

"Norman."

"Thank you. We'd like to ask you a few questions regarding your knowledge and whereabouts. Can you tell us where each of you were on the evening of August 29 between the hours of 8:00 p.m. and 9:00 p.m.?" Hilda asked.

Simon shrugged. Hermon turned to Simon, then to Norman, then lowered his eyes to his lap without a word. Norman stared straight ahead at Hilda like a rock.

"What about," she checked her notes, "August 1?"

Hermon squeaked, but said nothing and continued to stare into his lap. Simon and Norman said nothing.

"Okay, how about September 14..." Still the three looked like statues.

"October 3? November 1?" Hilda said in frustrated anger, but the three brothers did not say a word.

"You realize by not answering our questions, you are obstructing this investigation," she blurted.

...

...

...

"Well, then maybe you can tell me if you recognize these items," she added, setting the plastic bags filled with the ornate sickle that matched Simon's hat and the shovel that matched the hue and tone of Hermon's hat.

...

...

...

"Still nothing? See these pictures," she said, laying out pictures of the poor tie-dyed shavings of the polar bears, the field of poles, the shreds of Santa's suit and the frozen pumpkins that turned to mush on the front page of the *Washington Post*, all in a line in front of the gnomes.

...

Norman unsuccessfully held back a chuckle.

...

"Really...you have nothing to say?" she replied.

...

...

Simon sniggered.

"Fine, maybe a little time behind bars will jog your memory," Hilda said, grabbing the evidence bags and pictures and shoving them all into the file folder before leaving the room with her tape recorder.

Cupid eyed each of them for a moment before following her out the room.

"Oh, those little creeps are definitely not telling us what they know."

"Obviously...they haven't said a word."

"Don't get snarky with me. I'm not in the mood," Hilda said, slamming the file on the top of an unsuspecting bookcase.

"May I make a suggestion?"

"Sure, why not," she said, out of patience.

"I think we should let them stew for a while. Let them mull over all the items we've shown them and then put them each in separate interview rooms next time we speak to them. I have a feeling we might be able to break one of them if they think the others have spoken up, maybe we can beat them at their own game."

"I like it," she said with a most devious smile that made Cupid a little fearful. "Okay...Officer Agatha...please escort our guests to individual cells and let them sit there for a while," Hilda commanded.

"Yes, ma'am," she retorted dutifully.

"In the interim, I'm going to see if I can renegotiate with the reindeer on behalf of Santa," Cupid alerted Hilda.

"Good luck with that. Reindeer are incredibly stubborn," Hilda offered.

"So I've heard," Cupid said.

On the way to the stables, a siren blared alerting the small community something was amiss in the factory. Fairies, groggy elves, and a mosh posh of magical beings were running every which way. Cupid was distracted by the commotion and ran right into Santa lugging a huge sack of something, knocking the two men into a pile in the snow atop the bag.

"I'm sorry, Cupid, I didn't see you," Santa said.

"Nor I. What's going on?"

"The candy cane machine."

"Oh?"

"The violet fairy thought she'd spice things up by changing the red and white canes to purple and pink. Guess she hadn't realized that candy canes from Santa mostly come in red and white. Can't blame her, though. You make the same thing for hours on end and sometimes your eyes just need something different to look at. I'm sure we can offer them to the Easter bunny for baskets in the spring. They won't go to waste, but it's not exactly helping our deadline."

"Well, at least it wasn't another elven caper," Cupid offered.

"True. Hey, since I ran into you, could you do me a favor?" Santa asked.

"Of course. I was just heading to the stable to try to talk some sense into the reindeer. What do you need?"

"This sack. I need you to swap it out for the bag you saw in the kitchen and take it to the barn and label it POISON or something just as noticeable. Also, check the other sacks in storage by sampling them to make sure there are no more sugar substitutes in there. If there are, label them the same as the other. I want to get the elves back to feeling themselves and on track."

"Good idea. I'd be happy to do that."

"Great. The sooner, the better."

"Right. I'll head to the kitchen straight away."

"Thanks, Cupid. You've been a big help," Santa said, patting him on the back, but making sure not to crush his wings before scurrying off to fix the candy cane machine.

Chapter Nine

It was obvious after only a few seconds with Dasher that Cupid would not be making any headway with the reindeer, which he found very disappointing. If they did indeed succeed in producing all the toys needed, got them wrapped and packed, they'd still be a useless pile of stuff if they couldn't get them delivered.

He was pondering this when a fairy flitted by, leaving a glittery trail behind that glinted in the light then subtly disappeared. *Hmm*. Cinderella's godmother transformed mice into horses to get her to the ball, maybe something similar could work. He stopped a witch that was delivering a box of items to the factory.

"Excuse me, could I ask you a question?"

"Of course, if it doesn't take too long. I promised I'd get this box of rubber pellets to the doll machine as soon as I could," she stated.

"This won't take but a minute. Hypothetically, could other animals be used to say, fly a sleigh to deliver presents?"

"That's not very hypothetical when we all know there's an issue with the reindeer." Cupid shrugged at the remark.

"But, I suppose, yes, to a degree. You'd be better off just

making the animal able to fly and not changing it into a reindeer."

"Why's that?" Cupid asked.

"Simplicity. The simpler the spell, the less likely for it to go awry. I assume you're referring to something like the Cinderella story?"

"Yes."

"Okay, well, in that situation, obviously the mice would not be able to pull a carriage, hence the necessity for changing them into horses. Plus, a small animal like a mouse doesn't have the stamina for something as arduous as pulling a sleigh around the world.

"Now, if you were to use an animal that is similar to a reindeer—already large, strong and capable of a long journey—then gave it the ability to fly, you might have a feasible transporter."

"Interesting. So you're saying a deer, or maybe even a moose, might be a possible substitute?"

"Possibly. I don't know how the Christmas magic works on the reindeer, but if it too could be used along with a little help from other magic, it's very likely."

"Thank you so much for your input. I'll let you get back to your work, but I might need to talk to you at a later time, if Santa thinks this might be a feasible stand-in for the reindeer."

"No problem."

"Great." The witch turned and headed on her way. This was great news. He may not have had any luck with Dasher and his team but having a backup plan might just make this Christmas actually happen.

He raced off to talk to Santa about the idea. He rehearsed his speech in his mind as he made his way. It sounded good, but he often thought his ideas were good until the words came out of his mouth. Santa had a lot riding on this. He didn't want to sound too farfetched or not thought out. For this to work, many things would have to align perfectly and as he learned from experience, dealing with magic was never foolproof.

He was huffing and puffing when he knocked on Santa's door. He was met by Clara and a delicious smell of freshly-baked cinnamon buns that delighted his nose and made his tummy growl.

"Cupid."

"Clara, is Santa available for a quick chat?"

"Of course, come in." She invited him inside, pointing the way to the living room where he found Santa with his nose deep in a giant book."

"Have a moment, Santa?"

"Uh," Santa looked up, taking his glasses off. "Just a few. I'm going through the naughty and nice list for the first time this season. Usually by this time, I'd be on my second pass, but, well, you know."

"Yes."

"Did you get that sweetener swapped out for the sugar?"

"I did, and checked the other bags for more. I couldn't find any, so our perpetrators must have brought the bag themselves."

"Makes sense as the elves would never purchase it on their own."

"Right."

"And the reindeer?"

"I spoke to Dasher, but as you had said, he wasn't having any of it."

"Yeah...I figured as much," Santa said with a sigh of disappointment.

"However, I may have an alternative to the reindeer."

Santa looked surprised. "Really? What's that?" he said with interest.

Cupid carefully explained the conversation he'd had with the witch, covering as much detail as he could while Santa listened intently. Clara came in with a plate of warm decadence and two small plates for each of the men, before sitting to listen to the plan Cupid painted for them.

When he was done, Santa was silent as he munched on his treat. Clara looked from Cupid to Santa and then back to Cupid once more.

"What a clever plan," she said then looked to Santa for support.

"I'm sorry. Yes, it's an interesting proposal, but tricky, too. The reindeer have adapted to the magic they endure every Christmas Eve through their long line of ancestors who came before them, but immersing a different species could bring more surprises than it's worth. However, with no other option in hand, we may have to resort to unpredictable and just pray all works out in the end."

"We knew it would be a stressful Christmas Eve going into it," Clara offered.

"True, and it most often is without our present predicament, making my asking so many to take on an evening of such perturbation even harder. I can't offer anyone anything but my heartfelt thanks for their work thus far and I just seem to keep adding to their pile of work and sacrifice."

"They understand the situation, Santa. They don't expect compensation. They're doing it because of the children and the joy you brought them when they were small and awaited your coming. Don't be so hard on yourself. I can't speak for the others but I know for me, I want to help. I may have come here on a job, but I'm staying because I want to help."

"That's very kind of you, Cupid," Santa said as Clara rubbed his shoulders.

"Chin up, sir. If nothing else, we have a backup plan in the event the reindeer continue on with this strike."

"Right," Santa tried to say enthusiastically but failed miserably.

With fewer than two weeks left until Christmas Eve, things around the little town were humming like a well-tuned machine. After swapping out the sweetener for the sugar, slowly the elves seemed to be behaving more and more like elves should. They were working hard with the magical creatures to make ends meet for their December 24th deadline.

Unfortunately, the gnome brothers had been released soon after their detainment. There was no definitive proof the tiny men had finagled the disastrous pranks of the last few months. Hilda was beside herself. She had questioned them individually as Cupid had suggested and though Hermon looked about to have a nervous breakdown from the incessant interrogation, he corroborated his brothers' stories and left Hilda's hands tied.

Their only hope was to catch them holding a smoking gun, so to speak, but so far, that hadn't happened. It would be hard to keep an eye on the crabby men while working in the factory, but Cupid had faith they'd make a mistake and he'd be there to see it. Hilda, on the other hand, was not as confident and grumbled every time the gnomes were mentioned in passing.

"You've got to let this go, Hilda. We'll catch them. I have no doubt."

"I wish I had your confidence, Cupid."

"But in the meantime, look at all that has been accomplished. Most of the elves have gone back to work and continue to make progress toward the goal. The reindeer have even been less obstinate since the elves have gone back to their duties in the stables."

"You're one of those 'everything's sunshine and rainbows' kind of people, aren't you?"

"I like to be optimistic in my approach, if that's what you're getting at."

She rolled her eyes at him and scanned the file folder labelled Norman Gnomez.

After his talk with Hilda, Cupid headed back to the factory to see if there was anything he could do to help. Of course, there was, and after putting in a good six hours of working in quality control testing toys, he was ready to eat and call it a night.

It was late when he made it back to the hotel and all was quiet. The front desk was elfless as was the restaurant, which he found odd. The kitchen had been open twenty-four hours since the elves were off the sweetener to keep the factory employees working around the clock fed. He stepped into the kitchen from the hall door he had used once before and found the back door ajar and an elf passed out on a sack labelled "Flour."

The tiny elf snored softly, twitching much like you might see a dog doing as he dreamed of chasing critters. Had the sugar been switched out, or was the elf just taking a short nap? He wasn't sure. There were plenty of baked items all around the kitchen in different stages of cooling, therefore the elf had been extremely busy, but there was no way of determining if the sleeping was from sweetener intoxication or not. The elf looked so content, Cupid decided to let him sleep, but he did take a sample of sugar for the lab, just to make sure.

He heard something outside and snuck over to the back door, being careful not to make the floorboards squeak under his weight. He took a peek. It was a strange view indeed. A sack was on a small sled that was moving away from the door, drawing two parallel lines behind it in the snow. It looked to be moving on its own until Cupid noted tiny footprints between the lines that moved away from him.

Cupid kept out of sight and followed the sled. Could it be one of the Gnomez brothers swapping out the sugar again? It certainly seemed so since on occasion he caught a glimpse of a small hat when the sled made a turn. In the dark, he couldn't determine the color of the hat, for that would ultimately determine which brother it was.

He opted to keep following the sleigh to see where it led. He was thankful he had grabbed a handful of warm cookies and put them in his parka pocket before venturing into the cold, or his growling stomach would give him away to the perpetrator he was in pursuit of.

He kept his distance and nibbled on the yummy concoctions, never taking his eye off the moving object. It seemed liked they walked a mile. It was windy and flurries of white snowflakes would temporarily block his sight of his target, but it did help to hide him from view of the possible villain. The bad thing was the snow was filling in the tracks from the sled and the little man. That said, the tracks Cupid had made in stalking the little man had also been covered and he was counting on that trail to show him the way back to the hotel.

There was a giant pine he had spied in the distance in front of them when they were near the stables and it seemed they were heading for it. The tree grew larger as they drew nearer and nearer.

After passing the last of the stables, it became harder and harder to find an obstruction to hide behind. In order to keep hidden, he had to let the distance grow between them. As he predicted, the tree was their destination. The tree seemed to be at the top of a small hill. He could barely make out the tiny figure as it approached a round entrance hole burrowed beneath the tree.

When the sled and its owner disappeared into the tunnel of snow, Cupid made his way nearer. On closer inspection, the tree was atop an embankment. Peering into the hole in the snow, Cupid could see a good-sized red, round door at the end. A tiny window in the door trickled warm light into the burrow.

There was no way Cupid could enter the domicile. The door was maybe three feet in diameter. He wasn't sure he could reach the door to knock on it, even if he crawled on his stomach into the snowy hole.

The low hanging branches of the tree lay on the piles of snow. Cupid tried to get under the branches to see if there might be a window to the house, but he was moving the branches so much that a huge blanket of snow fell from high above, completely covering him, and it was a good thing, too, for he could hear voices that had come out to investigate the ruckus Cupid had been making. Determining the noises Cupid had made were that of the wind, the little men retreated back into their comfy home.

When the coast was clear, Cupid proceeded to dig his way out of the snow. While not knowing which direction he was going, his numbing hands scraped against something solid and suddenly there was a glimmer of light in the darkness.

He'd dug to a tiny window of glowing warmth. Being careful not to reveal too much of the window thus showing himself, he peered in. There he saw the three little gnome brothers surrounded by bags marked *sweetener*. They were shoveling it into bags labelled *Sugar*. Shivering in the coldness, Cupid grabbed his cellphone and made sure the flash was off before taking a photo through the tiny access.

He had his evidence. It was time to make it back to civilization and the warmth of the hotel and his bed. Grunting, complaining, cussing and crying, he turned himself around in the tunnel he'd dug, getting stuck once when his tiny bow got caught on a branch that had been buried in the snow.

He wriggled and moved until he was finally released, though he was quite sure his movements caused a bit of an avalanche behind him. Thankfully the snow was not excessively wet and was very powdery and easy to dig. Determined to break free of his snow tomb, he dug upward, the ceiling giving way allowing in a strong wind, making Cupid shiver.

Cupid had a long walk back with no visible sign of his footprints. After a dozen paces, Cupid looked backward to make sure the tree was to his back, but after half an hour of this feat, the tree blended in with the darkness of the sky and brushed clean by the swirling snow-laden gusts of wind.

He pulled the hood of his parka tighter to his face, adjusted his scarf over his nose and mouth and jammed his frozen, gloved hands deep into his pockets. He progressed slowly as the snow grew deeper and deeper. The weight of his body plummeted through the fluffy frozen powder, making every step a gigantic effort.

He was exhausted and couldn't feel his extremities, yet still there was no sign of the stables or lights from the small city. He wondered if he would die out here in the cold to be found by a passerby after the storm.

He tried to focus on the warm cookies and the hot stove of the hotel kitchen, but with each step, he found it harder and harder to think on such things when he was so tired. Not long after, he succumbed to his fatigue and fell to the soft ground in slumber.

Even his dreams would not relieve him of the cold. He found himself at the Lagoon of Ice looking upon the brightly-colored and shaved polar bears he'd seen with Santa. He could hear a faraway rumble that seemed to be getting closer until it was almost deafening. That could only be one thing, Hilda's snowmobile.

He could see the blue-eyed troll coming toward him but he couldn't hear her words. Something grabbed him. He wondered if he'd been attacked by a polar bear while being distracted by Hilda. He was suddenly upside down and something hard was against his stomach. Was he bouncing? He couldn't tell. The polar bear must have been throwing him around when he heard that godawful droning noise once more. The air smelled of gasoline and engine oil as the noise deafened him.

Warmth. Was it warmth? Yes. His butt seemed tingly, burning and vibrating and something big and soft was against his back. He wondered if the polar bear was being amorous and hoped he was wrong, continuing to focus on the pin needles burning in his butt and permeating outward to his gut, back, and thighs. It hurt, but it also felt kind of good.

With that thought, everything went black and all was quiet and warm.

Chapter Ten

Cupid woke to find himself warm in his bed, though his hands, feet, and face burned something fierce. In the room with him was Mrs. Kringle and Hilda.

"Oh good. You're awake," Mrs. Kringle said with a sigh of relief.

"Where...how did I get here?"

"Hilda found you on her rounds last night not far from the stables, and it's a good thing she did, another few minutes and you might have been dead."

"I..." he started.

"What in the world were you doing out in the storm like that?" Hilda demanded.

"I...I was following..."

"Following? Following what?" Hilda asked.

"Sack of...tree...gnomes..."

"You need to rest, Cupid. You're not making any sense," Mrs. Kringle encouraged.

"No. He needs to tell me what he's talking about."

"It can wait, Hilda," he heard Mrs. Kringle tell her as she shuffled the giant woman out of the hotel room.

"But," Hilda said before he heard the door shut.

"Just rest, Cupid."

He smiled and slipped into a deep, contented sleep.

Cupid opened his eyes and found an elf woman changing bandages on his bright red and chapped hands.

"Aw. Mr. Cupid. Good to see you awake," she said.

"I...where's Mrs. Kringle? he asked.

"She's working in the factory, but she stops by on her breaks to check on you, as does the giant police woman on occasion."

He was confused by her comment. "How long have I been asleep?"

"Three days, Mr. Cupid."

"Three days?" he said in surprise and tried to throw back the covers but he couldn't grasp anything with his bandaged hands. He looked at them puzzled.

"What's going on?"

"You were found in the snow in the storm. We thought you might die, but you didn't," the elf said bluntly.

"I need to speak to Santa right away," he said, looking around the room for his parka then trying to stand and make his way to it. But his feet were bandaged, too, and it stung when the floor met the bottom of his feet, making him plop back into the bed.

"Your hands and feet are going to be sore for a while, but at least you didn't lose anything."

"Lose anything?"

"Yes. Extremities are the first to go in the cold...fingers, toes, feet, ears."

At the mention of each body part, Cupid's eyes widened

in surprised as he felt his hands and ears to confirm they were in fact intact.

"Stay put and I'll call the big man and tell him you would like to see him."

"Thanks," he said to the plain-spoken woman.

The elven woman had done as she promised, and within a few minutes, Santa knocked on Cupid's door. It had given him time to get dressed, assess all his bandages, and note in the mirror how lobster red his face was.

Opening the door, Cupid greeted Santa and Hilda.

"Santa."

"Good to see you up on your feet. You gave us quite a scare."

"Sorry about that. It hadn't occurred to me how far I had gone in following our perp."

"Then you have something for us?" Hilda asked excitedly.

"I do," Cupid said, reaching for the pocket of his parka and revealing his cell phone. He showed the intrigued onlookers the picture he had taken under the snow of the giant pine. The picture showed the bags of sweetener being swapped out for bags of sugar, a few hundred baked goods covering every flat surface in the hovel and the three gnome brothers amongst all the evidence.

"I realize the picture in and of itself is not plausible evidence that the Gnomezes are behind the switcheroo, but it will at least be enough to get a search warrant and bring them back in for questioning," Cupid admitted.

"This is awesome," Hilda applauded.

Santa showed no excitement, in fact, he looked rather sad as he took in all the details of the photo. "Might I have the opportunity to speak with the brothers?" Santa asked Hilda while handing the phone back to Cupid.

"Well, it's not protocol, but then again, you are the boss up here, so I don't see why not."

"Thanks. I better get back to work," Santa said.

"Me, too," Hilda said, grabbing the doorknob.

"Thank you both for your dedicated efforts to apprehend our wrongdoers. They'll certainly be put on the Naughty List this year," Santa relayed.

"No doubt, see ya!" Hilda said, practically running out of the room.

"Santa. Are you all right?"

"Yes. It just saddens me that Norman, Simon, and Hermon would do such a thing. Makes me wonder what I've done to make them so angry."

"The gnomes don't seem to be what I would call a 'happy' bunch to begin with."

"They can be."

"Oh? Is that why you want to talk with them?"

"Yes. Maybe somehow this whole thing can be worked out."

"You are a generous man, Santa."

"Not really. I just believe there is good in beings and that it's circumstance that brings forth the anger and fear that is acted upon against our innate goodness."

"Hmmm."

"Anyway. Like I said, I better get back to it."

"Of course, sir. Goodbye."

The next day, Hilda contacted Santa as promised for him to question the criminals. Santa was solemn when he entered the police station.

"Good to see you, sir," Hilda greeted him. Cupid entered the building behind Santa and Hilda nodded a hello to him.

"I'm glad you're both here. The brothers refuse to speak as they did before. They've got me pulling my hair out. Maybe you two will have better luck than me," she admitted.

"Perhaps," Santa said as she led both men into the interrogation room where all three little men sat handcuffed to the table. They looked to be surprised to see Santa among them and looked between themselves for an answer, but none of them offered one.

"Norman. Simon. Hermon," Santa said, seating himself at the table and adjusting his beard.

The gnomes nodded in unison and mumbled, "Santa," in humble greeting.

"It's come to my attention that you are behind the drugging of elves and shenanigans that have wreaked havoc on our Christmas schedule."

Hermon held back a quiet sob and refused to look Santa in the eyes.

"I would just like to know what brought you to such a dark place that you could endanger the delivery of presents to the little boys and girls around the world. Are you angry with me? Have I offended you in some way that you felt it necessary to do such things?"

Hermon sniffled and wiped at his eyes, but Norman and Simon were still.

"I've known you all your lives, boys, please, let me know what has caused such a rift between us."

Simon spoke. "You know how we gnomes feel about slavery, and yet you enslave our cousins, the elves, day in and day out to do your bidding. What kind of man forces tiny people to work like that?"

"You are misinformed, my dear Simon. The elves are not my

slaves, in fact, they consider it an honor to work here. They don't think of themselves as working for me but working for the children they make toys for. I am just the distributer of their generous labor of love," Santa explained.

Simon retorted, "You provide them with no income to live on, that is the very definition of slavery."

"There are more ways to pay a being for their efforts than money. Gnomes are not paid for their efforts as guardians of gardens. We provide homes for the elves to live and thrive in. They have jobs they enjoy and love and most importantly, we consider them family. I love and respect each and every one of them as if they were my own children."

"You do?" Simon said, surprised.

"I do. We, Clara and I, celebrate every birth and mourn every death. We share meals with them and work side by side with them. Ask them yourselves, and if you find one that is unhappy, send them my way. I'd like to fix that, but I think you will find they are quite content."

Hilda blurted an addition, "How can you condemn Santa for slavery when you drugged them and made them do things they would never normally do?"

Simon stumbled over his response. Cupid wondered if he had never looked at the pranks in that light. "We...I...that wasn't...Norman, we've become what we abhor," he blurted. Hermon whimpered.

Norman eyed Santa. "Nonsense, Simon. The giant woman is just twisting our words to her advantage." Hilda sneered at his comment.

"You say you're all about family, Santa...what about our family?"

"What about it?"

"Gnomes thrive in a society of gnomes, yet do you see any gnomes here aside from the three of us?"

"No, but there was once a great bunch of you here."

"Indeed there was, once upon a time, but no more."

"True enough. I have noticed the decline."

"Well, how observant of you," Norman jibed. "Our family has died off to just us three. We've implored others to come here, but let's be serious, what is there to offer them? We serve no purpose here. We can't garden under all this snow, which I might mention is year-round.

"We live on a glacier of ice, for god's sake. We live in an icy hole in the ground under one of very few trees in the area. We stand day and night outside the stable gates and the town center, but there are no plants that can survive the harsh weather here, yet we do our job without complaining, as depressing as it is."

"I had no idea, Norman. Why haven't you or your ancestors before you ever mentioned this to anyone?"

"It's not our way. It is not in our nature to snivel or belly ache about things."

"I'm sorry, Norman, Simon, and Hermon, but sometimes you must make your concerns known. Though we are all magical beings, I do not read minds. You should have come to me much, much sooner. We could have figured something out. No one should have to live under conditions they despise. How can I make life more enjoyable for you?"

"Get rid of all this snow," Norman said.

"I think you know I can't do that. It is the way of life here at the North Pole."

Cupid jumped in saying, "Santa...I might have an idea." He whispered something in Santa's ear that led to a twinkle in the old man's eye and a smile on his face.

"Gentlemen, might I get back to you on this?" Santa asked the gnomes.

"It's not like we're going anywhere," Norman said, yanking at the handcuffs connected to the table.

"About that...Hilda, release them."

"What? I can't do that."

"Aren't I the boss?"

"Well, yes," she said, confused.

"I'm not pressing charges, so I ask that you let them go."

"But they cut up your suit. They terrorized the polar bears. They stole all those pumpkins."

"I'm aware of what they did, Hilda. Now would you please uncuff them and let them go home," Santa said sternly. Hilda was not happy, but she did what Santa asked. The gnomes were confused but they rubbed their wrists and shuffled out of the room before someone decided otherwise.

"Cupid, come with me," Santa said, holding the door for him.

Chapter Eleven

Santa pulled a team of elves and fairies away from the factory and explained the happenings of his conversation with the gnomes. With their help and under the supervision of Cupid, they went straight to work on Cupid's plan. It wasn't the greatest time to have extra hands working on a project other than the Christmas deadline, but Santa felt sure that he and Cupid had found a solution for both problems.

December twenty-first, all was completed and a moose-pulled sleigh was driven to the giant pine tree on the snowy bank Cupid had once snuck upon. Santa manned the sleigh himself and invited the brothers to join him for an early Christmas surprise. The unsure gnomes piled into the sleigh next to Cupid and they headed back to town.

They were greeted by every elf, reindeer, moose, magical being, and Clara. They were deposited near the town center where a large glowing structure had been erected. The crowd made a path to a door of what looked to be an ice-laden glass house. It was impossible to see in, but it gave off a warm glow.

"Gentlemen," Santa said as he opened the door and a fog billowed out into the frigid air.

The men timidly stepped in, feeling a burst of warmth as they entered. Cupid and Santa followed them in. Inside the glass building were green plants, red plants, small plants and large. It was like a tropical oasis in the middle of the North Pole. A tiny stream flowed through a garden. A pebble path mimicked the water's edge.

"What is this?" Norman asked.

"This is your garden."

"But..."

"No buts, no obligations. This is for your people. I expect with something like this, you will be able to recruit more gnomes to our icy town?"

"Well, yes, but..."

"My only request is that if you ever feel as you did before, that you come to me before you take matters into your own hands."

Hermon stood admiring his surroundings, touching leaves as if making sure they were not a mirage or a figment of his imagination. Simon, with his mouth open in awe, just looked around.

"Thank you," was all Norman could say.

"Oh, there is one other thing," Santa said.

"Hmm?" Norman said.

"Would you be willing to offer your services to the children of the world?" Santa asked.

"How?" all three gnomes said in unison.

"Could you use your growing magic to offer gifts to the kids?"

Simon said, "You mean like growing Venus fly traps for boys and miniature roses for girls?"

"Exactly," Santa said.

"Are you kidding? Of course, we would. It would be our pleasure," Norman replied. Hermon just sobbed in happy tears with his hands clasped together.

"Perfect. We only have two days to get all this done. Thank you for your help, boys."

"Thank you, Santa!" they said together, smiling widely—a sight Cupid had never seen before.

Santa patted Cupid on the back as they turned toward the door to get back to work. "Nice work, Cupid, and an excellent idea you had in coming up with the greenhouse for the brothers."

"Thanks, Santa. Just trying to do my part."

"You have, and then some," Santa said. It warmed Cupid's heart to see Santa happy and the case solved.

As the two emerged out of the warmth of the greenhouse into the chilly arctic air, they were greeted by gasps of fear from the crowd of elves.

"What is it?" Santa asked a nearby elf.

"Listen," he said.

They did, and they heard a boom that shook the ground, then another and another. They grew louder with each rumble. The roofs of the buildings vibrated, moving huge amounts of snow to piles on the ground. The ice sculpture of Santa in the center split down the middle in creaks and cracks in response the resonance.

Closer and closer it came and many of the elves fled the area, others stood behind Santa and Cupid for protection from whatever seemed to be coming their way.

Cupid heard a familiar noise. It was the deafening sound of one snowmobile whining under the massive woman who rode it. Behind her were giant figures lumbering and appeared to be the responsible for the crashing reverberations they heard. Hilda drove up in a blur of snow and clamor.

"What is this, Hilda?"

"The trolls. They've come. Remember a while back I had told you I'd put out a call for my troll kin to come help? Well, we are a slow bunch, be we are dependable. Troll magic is the most powerful magic in the world—though I may be a little biased." Hilda winked.

"Well, the more the merrier. Thank them for coming and have them see the head elf for direction in how they can help."

"You bet, sir," Hilda said. She waved her arm in the air to the giants behind her and she blasted off toward the office of the head elf.

"Looks like things are looking up, Santa," Cupid offered.

"It does, doesn't it?" Santa answered.

The next two days were a harmonious exercise of different beings coming together for one common cause— the children of the world. The gnomes propagated many clever and beautiful plants for little ones and were so proud to be useful during the Christmas crunch when before, they were always just observers. They understood why their cousin elves devoted their tasks and talents to such a noble cause. They were truly happy for the first time in a long time.

The elves worked tirelessly beside the witches, fairies, and other magical beings to accomplish the amazing undertaking of constructing toys for every girl and boy on this pretty blue marble we call home. The trolls did the heavy lifting, making things go faster than just the one crane the elves had for production. It was their extra magic, or maybe their presence just scared the reindeer into accepting, either way, they were finally on board for the Christmas Eve delivery flights.

If they hadn't all come together despite their differences, Christmas would not have come this year, but thankfully with the help of Cupid solving the case of the "Elves Gone Wild" and rolling up the sleeves of his pink union suit and lending a hand, all the children received their gifts December twenty-fourth and all was right in the North Pole.

As Santa made his way home that night, those famous words he always proclaimed were more heartfelt than in the years gone past. "Merry Christmas to you all...and to all a good night!"

Epilogue

"And that's how Christmas was saved," the woman ended her story. The youngest had drifted off to sleep and the oldest lay wide-eyed, sucking on the pink and purple candy cane her grandmother had given her as a treat while she recited the tale.

"Did that really happen, Grandma?" the young girl asked as the grandmother deposited a pink and purple candy cane under her sister's pillow.

"I couldn't say, sweetpea. I'm just relaying a story my grandmother told me, once upon a time. Now, it's time for sleep so Santa can come," she offered.

"You mean if the elves didn't go crazy and the reindeer didn't go on strike this year?"

"That's right, sweetpea. Goodnight," she said at the door before turning out the lights.

"Night, night, Grandma. I love you."

"I love you, too. Night, night."

The End

About the Author

T. Lynne Tolles can be found most days, juggling one of two cat muses and a laptop, tripping over a Newfoundland puppy and washing a never-ending pile of laundry. When life doesn't get in the way, she writes paranormal romances for new adults.

Her passion for witches, ghosts, and vampires together with a light-hearted wit are reflected in her loveable characters and the adventures of mystery they unravel to find their happily ever after.

Website:
https:tlynnetolles.me

Other Books by T. Lynne Tolles

Somber Island

Mirror of Shadows

BLOOD SERIES BOOKS

Prequel: The Hunted

Blood of a Werewolf

Blood Moon

Blood Lust

Bloodstone Heart

Deadman's Blood

Sisters in Blood

HELLHOUND TAILS BOOKS

Finding Midnight

Autumn Calls

For more info about T. Lynne Tolles and these books, check out her website.

tlynnetolles.me

www.ingramcontent.com/pod-product-compliance
Lightning Source LLC
Chambersburg PA
CBHW070641130626
46555CB00006B/2652